KINGDOM COME

KINGDOM COME

MARTIN McCALL

COVER ILLUSTRATION BY

RUDOLPH BELARSKI

STEEGER BOOKS • 2019

CHAPTER I

ETCHED IN ACID

CORCORAN RUBBED THE stiff joint of his knee, his leg, rigid in its steel brace, sticking out straight in front of him as he sat in the chair behind his desk. It was an unconscious gesture with him, one that Dominick Vane, who sat opposite him, knew very well. There was action in the wind, and at such times Corcoran's lips would tighten and his fingers would explore the knee which would no longer bend. The knee kept him out of the action which had been the bread and meat of life to him until that day when a Chicago gangster's machine gun had shattered his leg beyond all repair. It was after that that John Corcoran had become head of the Investigation Division of the Department of Justice in Washington—the head of that body of men who have become nationally famous under the name of G-men.

Dominick Vane had been one of Corcoran's closest friends since the early days of the department. They had fought a dozen battles side by side, this curiously matched pair. Corcoran was a short, stocky, two fisted, fighting Irishman; while Vane was tall, slim, dark with the hard, lined face of a man who had been to hell and back, despite the fact that he was not yet thirty-five. You knew this when you looked into his cold blue eyes that scarcely ever showed any warmth or emotion; a silent man, apparently without nerves, yet with a habit of smoking an endless chain of cigarettes which he consumed with furious rapidity. You sensed, despite his outer calm and his low, soft speaking voice, an inner quality of explosiveness, like that of a seething volcano.

"You look all in, Nick," Corcoran said.

Vane made an impatient gesture with his hand. "It's nothing that a little sleep won't put right. The last few days have kept me on the run."

Corcoran smiled gently. The last few days had seen the capture of the Scorsi kidnaping gang, and it had been Vane who, single-handed, broke into the mountain cabin where they were hiding and shot the three Italian murderers to death. Vane had been too impatient to wait for reïnforcements!

"Of course you should have a week off to get yourself rested up," Corcoran said, "but... well, something's turned up that I would rather have you handle than anyone else we have available."

"Shoot!" said Dominick Vane, and lit a fresh cigarette from the stub of the one he'd been smoking.

Corcoran leaned forward and picked up a sheaf of papers and clippings that lay on his desk. "I know you haven't been reading the papers the last few days," he said, "and even if you had you

might not have paid any attention to this story." Corcoran made as if to pass the papers to Vane but the latter leaned back in his chair and closed his eyes.

"Tell me about it yourself, Corky. That way we'll skip the unimportant details."

"It's a queer story," said Corcoran. "On the face of it, it wouldn't seem to be up our alley. Three nights ago—about two in the morning to be exact—a Jersey State Trooper was riding along the main highway near the town of Marshfield on his usual nightly patrol. As he turned a corner in the road his head-lights picked up the figure of a man lying in the ditch by the side of the road. This trooper, a guy named Hardwick, stopped his machine and went back to where the man was lying. Hardwick thought at first the man had been the victim of a hit-and-run driver. When he got to him the man wasn't dead. He groaned as Hardwick touched him and kept his face buried in the grass. Hardwick turned him over and… well, this fella didn't have any face!"

DOMINICK VANE'S eyes popped open and he said: "Why not, Corky?"

"Acid of some kind," said Corcoran. "Somebody had thrown it in this bird's mug and it had literally eaten away his face… eyes gone… the works! Hardwick told the local sheriff afterward that he nearly fainted when he looked at it. Well, this poor guy tried to talk, but he was coughing and choking and, before he could get anything out, he died."

Vane grunted and blew a spiral of smoke toward the ceiling. "Starts out like a dime novel," he said.

"It gets more like one as it goes on," said Corcoran grimly. "Trooper Hardwick sent for the Marshfield sheriff and the coroner. They came out and got the dead man, and the doctor concluded that the poor guy must have swallowed some of the acid… that was what killed him."

"Who was the dead man?" Vane asked.

"I'm coming to that," said Corcoran, and his voice had a hard ring to it. "They went all through his clothes and there wasn't a single thing to identify him by. But Hardwick figured it was murder. Somebody had thrown acid at this guy and it had killed him. There was a pretty clear trail through the swamps adjoining the highway where the dead man had staggered blindly to reach aid of some sort. Hardwick decided to back track on that trail in the hope of getting some clue to the murder. Though it was still dark he set out alone."

"Good man," said Dominick Vane.

Corcoran laughed mirthlessly. "Nobody heard from Hardwick for hours after that," he said. "In fact not till the next afternoon. About five miles from where Hardwick started out lives a rich young dope named Philip Jaxon, a nephew of H.R. Dawson, the big Wall Street operator. Young Jaxon doesn't do much but ride horses and drink. He plays around with a very fast set. That afternoon he was sitting on the terrace of his house having a highball when, suddenly, a man stumbled through the garden hedge. He started toward the house and fell flat on his face.

When Jaxon got to him he was unconscious. It was Hardwick. His uniform was torn to shreds. His gun was gone. And one of his hands—his right hand, to be exact—was almost eaten away by some strong acid."

"Ah," said Dominick Vane, and lit a fresh cigarette.

"They rushed him to a hospital," said Corcoran. "He was suffering from terrible internal injuries. Nearly all of the ribs on one side of his body were smashed and he was having internal hemorrhages. The doctors say he hasn't got a chance. They only hope they'll be able to bring him to before he dies—long enough for him to give them some idea of what happened. I had a report an hour ago. He was still unconscious."

"It's a nice case," said Dominick Vane, "but what has it got to do with the Department of Justice?"

"The local authorities sent us the fingerprints of the dead man—the one Hardwick found. They hadn't been able to identify him and they thought there might be a chance we'd have him on file. It was a ten strike. We had him all right."

"Who was he?" Vane asked.

Corcoran's voice was harsh. "Ted Drewes," he said.

Dominick Vane literally sprang out of his chair. "What are you talking about, Corky? Ted Drewes—dead! Why he—he's the best man your outfit ever had!"

"With the exception of yourself," said Corcoran grimly. "Oh, it's Ted all right enough. About four days ago he telephoned me from New York. He was up there on a job for us. He'd washed it up and was due back but he said he'd got on the trail of something very hot—something tremendously important. 'Biggest thing the department has ever been up against,' were his words. He didn't want to talk about it over the phone. He sounded all hopped up and wanted leave to work on his own hook for a day or two. I told him to go ahead."

"Quite right," said Vane grimly.

"And that was the last I heard from him, until these fingerprints came in." Corcoran shifted restlessly in his chair. "Ted wasn't the kind to go off half-cocked on a wild goose chase. If he said he was after something big he *was*. I want to know what that something is, Nick. And I want to know who got Ted!"

Dominick Vane was on his feet. "Have a car here to take me to Marshfield in ten minutes," he said, "with someone to drive me. I'll sleep on the way up." His eyes were cold and bright as diamonds. "Notify the hospital where this trooper is that I'm coming. I want to be on deck if he does any talking."

PAYING SCANT attention to speed limits, a Department car drove rapidly from Washington toward the town of Marshfield in Jersey. Sitting beside the driver Dominick Vane slept. Sleep was never a pleasant experience for this gaunt, hard-eyed agent of the Government, for it was always accompanied by a dream— a dream that brought out cold beads of perspiration on his forehead and wrenched his lips into a taut, suffering line. It was a dream that Dominick Vane had never been able to blot out since that terrible day five years ago when all the joy of living left him.

On that day Dominick Vane and his bride of two weeks had been standing arm in arm in front of a shop window on Fifth Avenue in New York. Dominick Vane was a promising lawyer, madly in love with the slender, lovely girl whose fingers clung to his arm so confidently, so happily. A touring car with drawn shades had come up the avenue. There had been a sudden roar of machine-gun fire. Instinctively Dominick Vane had drawn his wife into his arms to protect her… but she was dead, even as he looked down into her face….

The papers' account of the incident said:

MOB KILLING ON FIFTH AVENUE
JOE EMMANUEL KILLED BY
GUNMEN WHO ESCAPE

———

WOMAN ALSO SLAIN BY STRAY BULLETS

Woman also slain! Even in his sleep Dominick Vane could see those cold impersonal words. *Woman also slain!* That *woman* was Joan… his Joan! His life!

Dominick Vane had wanted to die, yet some iron streak in his character made it impossible for him to blow out his own brains. And while he struggled to get hold of himself that seething cauldron of fury began to bubble within him. A fury against every criminal, every gangster, every racketeer. It was as if he had a score to settle with each one of them. He joined the Department of Justice forces. Oh, he worked under orders from Corcoran, but each case on which he served was in reality to him a private war of vengeance. Dominick Vane succeeded where others failed because he took chances no other man would take. He wanted to die and, perhaps for that very reason, he lived….

Dominick Vane opened his eyes, and for a moment there was a tortured look in them—a look that was always there when he first came back to consciousness after sleep. It faded rapidly to be replaced by that diamond-hard, chill light that always glittered there whenever the chase was on. Ted Drewes had been a friend—a brilliant and fearless agent. Vane had a double score to settle in this Marshfield business.

"How much farther?" he asked the driver.

"Only about five miles, sir. You've slept all the way."

A few moments later they reached the town of Marshfield and were directed to the hospital. This proved to be no more than a large private house converted by the local doctor into a sort of sanitarium. Vane swung out of the car before it came to a full stop. "Wait!" he snapped at the driver and hurried up the porch steps to the entrance. A nurse in white starched uniform sat at a reception desk.

"You wish to see Doctor Tyler?"

"At once," said Vane. "He's expecting me."

"Doctor Tyler is engaged right now. If you'll—"

"At once!" Vane's voice had a whiplash quality to it. "I am from Washington."

"You're Mr. Vane?" she asked, with quickening interest.

"Stop asking questions and take me to Doctor Tyler!" said Dominick Vane.

At the same instant a door opened across the hall and a little gray man with rimless spectacles looked out.

"This is Mr. Vane, Doctor Tyler," said the flustered nurse.

"Mr. Vane… come in, come in. We're delighted to see you. It is something of an occasion for us to have a man of your reputation come to Marshfield. Of course we've all heard of your exploits, and I for one—"

"Has he talked yet?" Dominick Vane interrupted sharply, as the doctor closed the door of the office.

"No, Mr. Vane, I—ah—" The doctor, too, seemed flustered by the agent's cold, abrupt manner.

"What are the chances?" asked Dominick Vane.

Doctor Tyler shrugged. "There's no telling. Hardwick is terribly injured. He may die without ever recovering his senses."

"No delirium?" Vane asked. "No talk of any kind?"

"No," said the doctor. "There has been a nurse at his side ready to take down anything he might say, but up to now there has been nothing."

Dominick Vane lit a cigarette and sucked hungrily on it for a moment. "This acid, Doctor Tyler… what is it?"

The doctor looked down thoughtfully at the iodine stains on the fingers of his right hand. "Quite frankly, Mr. Vane, we don't knew."

"You've had three days to find out!"

"We've had the chief chemist from the State Laboratories here. He doesn't know either," said the doctor, a little tartly.

VANE LOOKED at Tyler sharply, and for just a second the hard lines at the corners of his mouth relaxed. "You'll pardon my abruptness, Doctor Tyler. Drewes, the murdered man, was a close friend of mine. If I could have got here at once… but after three days the trail to the murderer is already cold. I must know every possible fact relative to the crime, no matter how unimportant it may seem. Be good enough to send for the sheriff at once. I don't want to leave your hospital as long as there is any chance Hardwick may speak."

Doctor Tyler was not altogether a fool, and as he looked into the sharp, intense face of Dominick Vane his resentment faded. Here was a man very much on the job. Doctor Tyler approved of that sort of thing. He reached for the telephone on his desk and a moment later informed Sheriff Waters of Marshfield that Vane wanted to see him at once.

"This is a very strange case, Mr. Vane," said the doctor, turning from the phone. "You may know that we performed an autopsy on Drewes. In his case he had swallowed some of the acid which destroyed his face and eyes. It had literally eaten away his stomach, the lining of his throat, and part of the small intestine. In the case of Hardwick matters seem different. There is no sign of the acid having touched anything but his right hand. While his injuries are internal they have been caused by a terrible beating or a bad fall of some kind. If it were not for the mutilation of his right hand caused by the acid there would be no link between the two affairs. But, quite obviously, Hardwick came into close contact with the agency which caused Drewes' death. Those are all the medical facts in the case, Mr. Vane, and quite frankly I—"

The office door opened, interrupting the physician. A nurse poked her head in. "Hardwick is stirring, Doctor Tyler. Doctor Morgan thinks he may talk. He sent me to—"

Dominick Vane sprang out of his chair. "Hurry!" he said.

Trooper Hardwick lay in a bed in a private room on the second floor of the sanitarium. One look at him told Dominick Vane that the man was dying. The pallor of death was on his haggard face. But even as they entered the room his lips were moving swiftly.

Dominick Vane unceremoniously pushed aside the nurse and the young interne who were leaning over him and knelt by the head of the bed. But there was nothing rough about the way his cool hand closed over the left one of the dying man which lay on the coverlet. Hardwick was muttering unintelligibly.

"Try to speak a little more distinctly, old man," said Dominick Vane very gently.

Hardwick's fingers closed tightly about Vane's and his head moved restlessly on the pillow for a minute. Then very slowly and quite distinctly he said: "Men… hundreds of men… without faces…. Death… death everywhere."

Dominick Vane looked up sharply at Tyler, but the doctor shrugged. The trooper's words carried no significance for him.

"Where are these men?" Vane asked softly.

Once more the trooper's lips moved. "Hundreds of men… without faces… and… and a white-haired monster… horrible white-haired monster…. Oh, my hand… my hand… it's burning up… it's all burned to…" The lips stopped moving and the fingers relaxed their grip on Vane's hand.

"Where did this happen?" Dominick Vane asked, more sharply this time. But there was no response.

"I'm afraid he's gone," said Doctor Tyler, and his voice was a trifle unsteady.

CHAPTER II

COOK'S TOUR

SHERIFF WATERS OF Marshfield was waiting in Doctor Tyler's office when the physician and Dominick Vane returned from the room where Trooper Hardwick had just died. Waters was tall, paunchy, and decidedly rustic in appearance. He had never had any more serious crime to deal with than petty larceny or a drunken fight at one of the local road houses. He was impressed with meeting Dominick Vane, the famous government agent who had done for the Scorsi Brothers, but he did not want to appear overawed by the sharp-eyed Vane in the presence of Doctor Tyler. He listened judicially to the account of the death-bed scene.

"Sounds as though Hardwick had been hittin' the pipe," he said dryly. "Men without faces! White-haired monsters! That's crazy, Mr. Vane."

Dominick Vane was pacing restlessly up and down the office, a thin frown penciling his forehead. "Hardwick was trying very desperately to tell us what happened, Sheriff. It doesn't make sense now, but I'll bet you a five spot that when we get to the bottom of this it will." He paused in his pacing to light a cigarette.

"I'll take that bet," the sheriff laughed. "What do *you* reckon lies behind all this business, Mr. Vane?"

"I don't know," said Vane. "But this much I *do* know. Drewes was one of the shrewdest agents we had in the department. He told Corcoran, our chief, that he was on the trail of 'the biggest thing' the Department had been up against. The trail was hot, because he was brutally murdered. Hardwick accidentally stumbled across it, too, and he got his. I'm going to find out what Drewes was after, and I'm going to find out what Hardwick was talking about when he died."

"All most interesting and—ah—thrilling," said Doctor Tyler.

"Just part of the day's work for a G-man, eh, Mr. Vane?" said Waters, with a sage wink.

Vane paid no attention to either comment. "I want you both to cooperate with me in one respect," he said. "The criminal or criminals, whoever they are, probably know of my presence in Marshfield. They will naturally be anxious to know whether or not Hardwick told us anything before he died. I want you both to give out the report that he died without speaking."

"He might just as well have," said the sheriff.

"There is probably a definite key to the whole affair in what he told us if we can figure it out," said Vane. "I don't want anyone to know what he said. I want the criminals lulled into a sense of security. Is that understood, gentlemen?"

"Perfectly," said Doctor Tyler.

"And now, Sheriff, I should like to have you take me to the place where Drewes' body was found."

IT WAS a dismal spot on a deserted stretch of a great cement highway running south through the state. Both sides of the road were bordered by thickly grown marsh land. The sheriff chewed on a large cud of tobacco as he looked complacently down into a little grassy ditch.

"Drewes was lyin' here, face down in the grass, when Hardwick found him," he said. "Hardwick told me his fingers were sunk into the ground like he'd tried to pull himself up and couldn't. When I got here with the doctor, Hardwick had rolled him over on his back. But he was dead—died before we got here."

Dominick Vane's face looked as if it were hewn out of granite as he stared down at the spot where his friend had died. Then he looked out over the swamp land.

"I understood there was a pretty clear trail indicating which way Drewes had come," said the agent. "I see nothing now."

"The swamp grass was all stomped down," said the sheriff. "But it's rained since and it's all sprung up again."

"You made no attempt to follow it when Hardwick showed up—done in?" There was a caustic note of criticism in Vane's voice that made the sheriff shift his feet uneasily.

"Well, you see, I figured there was no use in that," he said. "I knew the murderer would be miles away by then."

"I see," said Dominick Vane. "You didn't think it worth while setting out after a man who had brutally killed two other men." He drew deeply on his cigarette and then flicked it away into the ditch. "What lies out there?" he asked, pointing to the dreary swamp land.

"Marsh fer about a mile," said the sheriff. "Then you come to the barrens."

"The barrens?"

"Pine barrens," said the sheriff. "Ain't nobody lives out there except a few half-wit squatters that've been there for years. Nobody bothers to kick 'em off because the land ain't good for anything anyway."

"Is this the only way to get there—through this swamp?"

"Oh, no. Up to the other end of town there's a sort of a road that goes in most of the way."

"Let's go," said Dominick Vane.

"You're goin' into the barrens?" the sheriff asked incredulously. His little eyes blinked.

"At once," said Vane.

"You won't get nothin' out of them people in there," the sheriff said. "They're all looney."

"Let's not waste any more time talking about it," said Vane.

THE SHERIFF drove his car in sulky silence. He wasn't accustomed to being dealt with quite so sharply. He was a person of importance in Marshfield and this government agent had no business ordering him around this way—even if he was a big shot.

Dominick Vane was far too absorbed with his own thoughts to take any notice of the other man's injured feelings. This was no ordinary murder case. Somehow Ted Drewes had got onto something of immense importance and had died in consequence. Yet why, if someone wanted to silence him, had they taken this clumsy method of throwing acid in his face and then let him go? If Hardwick had come on him sooner in that roadside ditch he might have been able to tell his whole story. And Hardwick, in turn, had been permitted to get away. He too had seen something. Hundreds of men without faces and a whitehaired monster! What *had* he seen? And who had killed him and Drewes? There was nothing—not a single clue of any sort as yet—to give even the faintest suggestion as to what lay behind the death of these two representatives of the law.

The sheriff broke in on Vane's reverie. "Young Jaxon lives over there," he said, pointing to a big, white colonial house set back from the road.

"Jaxon?"

"Sure. That's where Hardwick turned up. In Jaxon's garden. Lousy with money, young Jaxon is. Nephew of H.R. Dawson."

"Wait a minute," said Vane. "Let's go in and have a talk with young Mr. Jaxon before we go any farther, Sheriff. There may be something he can tell us. Hardwick may have said something, or Jaxon may have noticed something that would be of use to us."

"Blind alley there," said the sheriff. "I asked him plenty the day Hardwick turned up. He don't know anything."

"If you don't mind," said Dominick Vane coldly, "I'd like to do my own questioning."

"Say, look here…" The sheriff's face was beet red.

"That seems to be the entrance on the right," said Dominick Vane.

The sheriff swung the wheel of the car so sharply that they nearly skidded into one of the stone entrance gates. "I just want you to know, Mr. Vane," he said angrily, "that we aren't so dumb around here as you seem to think. If Jaxon had seen or heard anything he'd have told me. You can count on that."

"Lovely willow trees along this drive," said Dominick Vane.

"Okay, Mr. Wise Guy," said Waters. "We'll see just how smart *you* are." And he brought the car to a grinding halt before the magnificent entrance to Philip Jaxon's house. Vane had got a glimpse, as they came up the drive, of extensive stables at the back of the house. He remembered Corcoran saying that young Jaxon was something of a horseman.

A butler answered Vane's ring at the front door bell. "I'll see if Mr. Jaxon is at home," he said. Presently he returned. "If you gentlemen will come this way...."

THE BUTLER led them through a great entrance hall that ran the length of the house to a pair of French doors at the rear. Outside these doors was a flagstone terrace overlooking a lovely garden. There were two people on the terrace—a young man and a very pretty girl. Philip Jaxon sat sprawled in a wicker armchair, a highball glass in his hand. He was dark, brown as a nut, handsome in a sort of collar-ad way; a young man a little dissipated, a little too cynical for his own good, but with a very level pair of dark brown eyes that looked with interest at his callers. The girl too was dark, smart, brilliantly beautiful. The scarlet of her lips matched the flame colored tea gown she was wearing. She was vaguely familiar to Vane, who suddenly realized that he had seen her picture often in the rotogravure sections.

"Ah, Sheriff, sleuthing again?" Philip Jaxon drawled, without rising from his chair.

"Not today," said Waters. "I'm just conductin' a Cook's tour." He gave Vane a malicious lock. "This here is a Government agent from Washington who wants to ask you a few questions."

Jaxon threw up his hands in a mock gesture of surrender. "Don't shoot," he said. "I've paid my income tax."

"My name is Vane," said the agent dryly. "I want to ask you one or two questions about Trooper Hardwick."

"Not Dominick Vane, the scourge of the Scorsi boys!" cried Jaxon. "Angela, we were talking about Mr. Vane only this morning." The girl gave Vane a keen, interested look from beneath her dark lashes. Jaxon's voice had a note of respect in it. "That was a devilish brave thing you did, breaking in on those three murderous mutts single-handed! Sit down. Have a drink. Tell us about it."

"Can't you be polite in the presence of a national hero, Philip?" asked the girl. "Introduce me, please."

"Sorry," grinned axon. "Mr. Vane, this is Miss Angela Dawson who might be Mrs. Jaxon, except that she consistently refuses to marry me. But a Jaxon never fails to get his missus. Highball, Mr. Vane?"

"Thanks, no," said Dominick Vane. He was irritated. He hated any talk of his exploits, and he was in no mood for bantering. "Hardwick died about an hour ago," he said.

"Poor devil," said Jaxon. "They told me he didn't have a chance. Did he talk before he died?"

"No," said Vane. "I've come to see you in the hope that you can tell me something I don't already know. Something that you may not have recalled at the time Sheriff Waters questioned you."

"There isn't a blessed thing," said Jaxon. "Hardwick just stumbled into the garden there and collapsed. Never said a word. Of course you've figured it out, as I have, that whatever happened to him took place down in the pine barrens somewhere."

"Sure, we figured that out all right," the sheriff chimed in. "Mr. Vane is all for going down there but I tell him it's a waste of time. Them pineys won't be able to tell him nothing, and the murderer will be hundreds of miles away by now. And anyhow," he added as an afterthought, "it'll be dark in a couple of hours. We wouldn't be able to find anything out tonight."

"The sheriff's right, Mr. Vane. The pineys are a rum lot. You won't get much out of them," Jaxon said.

"None the less," said Vane acidly, "it seems rather elementary to me that in investigating a crime one shouldn't avoid the scene where it took place. I wouldn't bother you, Waters, but I would probably get myself nicely lost without a decent guide."

"Look here, Vane," said Jaxon with alacrity, "if the sheriff doesn't want to take you, I'd be delighted. I know that country like a book."

"Gosh, Mr. Jaxon, would you really?" said Waters eagerly. "There's business in town I ought to look after."

"What do you say, Vane?" Jaxon asked.

Dominick Vane hesitated a moment. Jaxon would undoubtedly be a better guide than the sulky sheriff. On the other hand, the pine barrens didn't seem to be a very healthy place for investigators at the moment. It was a risk he shouldn't let the young millionaire take.

"I used to know some of the pineys as a kid," said Jaxon. "They might even talk for me. But as I said, they're a rum lot. Undernourished, interbred for generations—they aren't very bright. A lot of 'em are albinos, you know."

"Albinos!" Vane's voice cracked sharply.

"Sure. White hair and pink eyes."

"Yes, I know," said Dominick Vane softly. He was thinking of Hardwick's last words. A *white-haired* monster!

It was then that Dominick Vane made a decision for which he was very grateful a little later. Jaxon knew the country; he even knew some of the pineys; he was eager to go. He would be a hundred times more useful than the antagonistic sheriff.

"Come along," Vane said, "if you really want to go with me, Mr. Jaxon."

Jaxon sprang out of his chair, his languid manner gone. "Great stuff," he said. "I've got a couple of electric torches in the house. We'd better have those because it will be dark before we get back."

"Have you got a gun?" Vane asked quietly.

"Sure. You think…?"

"I think you'd better bring it—just in case."

Angela Dawson looked up at Vane. "You think there's danger?" she asked.

"Drewes and Hardwick didn't find it exactly healthy," said Dominick Vane.

"There ain't nothing to worry about, Miss Dawson," said the sheriff. "It's like I said, the murderer will be hundreds of miles away by this time."

"Has it occurred to you, Waters, that he was still around a good many hours after he attacked Drewes? He was still there when Hardwick caught up with him. I'm not at all convinced that we won't find him there now!" Vane looked at Jaxon steadily. "I want you to understand that this may be no picnic."

"Fine!" said Jaxon. "I hate picnics."

CHAPTER III

SQUADS RIGHT

THEY WENT ON foot, for there was no adequate road into the Barrens. At first they talked a little. It was perhaps two miles to the nearest piney settlement, Jaxon told the agent. They had lived there for generations, these strange people, in a land where nothing would grow. How they kept body and soul together was a mystery. Completely illiterate these people were, with less contact with the civilized world than the Kentucky mountaineers, even though they were comparatively close to the greatest center of civilization in the world. They weren't vicious, Jaxon said, but childish in the extreme, utterly primitive in their point of view and in their way of life.

"A man could hide out among them for months and never be discovered," said Jaxon, "because nobody ever comes here."

And then, because Jaxon was sharing this adventure with him, Vane told him the whole truth; told him what Drewes had said to Corcoran. He told him of Hardwick's strange dying words: *"Hundreds of men without faces… and a white-haired monster!"*

Jaxon looked blankly at Vane. "It doesn't make any sense, does it?" And his voice echoed strangely in the cathedral-like silence of the great pine forest.

"The bit about the white-haired monster I think you've already explained to me," said Vance. "One of your albino pineys. If Hardwick saw him after he'd been injured the man might have seemed grotesque and horrible to him."

"Of course," said Jaxon, and he laughed a little nervously. "It has a very delirious sound to it—yet it might have been one of the pineys he saw. But… but the men without faces? What do you make of that?"

"Nothing… yet," Vane said.

And then he stopped walking. They had come into a sort of clearing and what he saw made Vane stare with a puzzled look in his eyes. The ground was pitted with holes—holes with earth and stone thrown about them.

"Now why the devil should anyone be digging holes out here in the middle of this waste?" Jaxon asked.

Vane went forward and stood on the edge of one of the pits. The muscles of his jaw rippled under the skin of his cheeks as he looked. Then he turned to Jaxon and asked, in a curious voice:

"How old are you, Jaxon?"

"Twenty-six. What the devil has my age got to do with it?"

"You were too young to have been in the war," said the agent. "I wondered. Because these, my friend, are *shell holes!*" He stopped and picked up a fragment of metal. "They were made by a small field piece of some sort."

"*Shell holes!*" Jaxon stared, utterly incredulous. "Vane, are you sure?"

"Positive," said Vane grimly. He looked up at the tree tops bordering the clearing. "From that direction," he said, pointing, "judging from the way the trees on that side are damaged."

"But what is anyone doing firing off a field piece out in this forsaken place?"

"That's what we'll have to discover," said Vane.

THEY STOOD in silence for a moment. Darkness was descending rapidly now, even there in the shell-pitted clearing. For a moment Dominick Vane had an overwhelming desire to turn back; for that one moment he was aware of a cautioning foreboding. It would be better to go back for more men, something told him. Ted Drewes had been unable to cope with the danger that lay ahead, and Drewes had had some inkling of what it was all about.

He drew a deep breath. "Game to go ahead?" he asked Jaxon.

"Why not?" said Jaxon. "Do we head in the direction from which these shells were fired or do we go toward the village?"

"I suggest the village," said Vane. "We may be able to get some direct information there that will save us a lot of guesswork."

They walked on for a bit. It was almost completely dark now. Jaxon took out the electric torch from his pocket.

"Use it as sparingly as possible," said Vane. "I haven't any particular desire to announce our coming."

They proceeded in silence, Jaxon flashing on the torch from time to time to spot some landmark he knew, for there was no clearly defined path now. Presently Dominick Vane stopped him, hand on his arm.

"Lights over to the right," he said. There was a rise in the land and from over beyond it a faint, flickering glow illuminated the trees and sky. It looked as if it might come from some sort of burning torch. Jaxon started to speak when from the distance came a voice, clear, metallic, sharp:

"Right by squads. March!" Then there was utter silence.

Vane and Jaxon stared at each other. Jaxon coughed. "Funny sickish smell in the air," he said. "Get it?"

Vane did. He got a whiff of some acrid stuff that seemed to burn the lining of his nose and throat.

"Column left. March!" came that metallic voice across the barrens.

"What is it?" said Jaxon. His voice sounded shaken.

"Let's head toward the light. We may be able to see something," said Vane. "Quiet as possible." And then he coughed, his throat burned by that unpleasant vapor that had suddenly pervaded the night air.

They moved on silently forward toward the glowing light that showed over the rise in the land and, as they moved, that strange metallic voice kept repeating a series of military commands. There was not another sound in the night. The air grew heavier with that sultry, sickish smell. Once they stopped while Jaxon choked back a strangling fit of coughing. No swamp ever gave off such acrid burning vapors as these, thought Vane.

As they approached the top of the rise in the ground, the glowing of the flickering light was much brighter… unquestionably from some sort of stationary torch. The commanding voice grew louder and yet there was no other sound, not even the crackling of a twig.

Then they reached the top of the hill.

Jaxon was the first to see, and his hand shot out and gripped Vane's arm so tightly his fingernails bit deep into the G-man's arm.

"Look!" he whispered, choking as he spoke. "The men without faces."

Vane looked. His lungs felt scorched. His eyes burned like fire. Yet he, too, saw. There was a wide square clearing over the brow of the hill. Stuck in the ground at various points were torches on the end of long sticks, giving a weird flickering light to the astonishing scene that lay before their eyes. Several hundred men were marching in military formation… there was not a sound as they trod on ground deep in a soft carpet of pine needles. *And they had no faces!*

SUDDENLY DOMINICK Vane found that he could not concentrate on this strange sight. His head was swelling up to an enormous size like a balloon, and then contracting until it seemed to him that the bones of his skull were going to be crushed. The whole scene wavered drunkenly before his eyes… the men were first enormously tall and then, an instant later, like distorted pygmies. Jaxon, beside him, suddenly began to laugh… mad, hysterical laughter.

Dominick Vane had one moment of clear thought left to him. Gas! And those marching men were wearing gas masks. And he and Jaxon were done for unless they got out fast! Drunkenly he staggered to his feet, grabbing Jaxon by the arm and yanking him to his feet.

"Run!" he said hoarsely. "Run for your life!"

Jaxon ran, laughing crazily. Vane plunged into the trunk of a pine tree, fell, struggled up once more and stumbled on. His lungs were on fire; tears were streaming from his scalding eyes. It was like some ghoul-filled nightmare. The sensation of swelling and contracting was growing more acute. Vane could hear the metallic voice of the commander of those masked troops shouting something that was now no more than a mad gibberish. Jaxon ran ahead of him, looking like a crooked figure reflected in a cracked mirror.

And then suddenly Vane fell… into a cool pond of still water. Jaxon was there ahead of him, sucking moisture into his tortured throat, bathing his seared eyes. The air was sweeter here. They must have run a long way. Vane, sick and dizzy, thought how easy it would be to sink under the cool surface of the water and die. Then he saw the monster… the thing that Hardwick, as he lay dying, had called the *white-haired monster!*

It crouched on the opposite bank of the pool, teeth bared in a diabolical grin. It was in the shape of a man, yet somehow the long white hair drooping down to the shoulders, the glittering little pink eyes, were like nothing human.

Yet it was a man. Vane heard Jaxon cry out:

"Furno! You know me! It's Philip Jaxon!"

The white-haired thing laughed—a horrible, gloating sound. In its hands it held a long brass tube which looked like a fire extinguisher. The plunger was drawn back and it was pointed at Jaxon.

"Furno fix so no one know you!"—A frightening falsetto voice—frightening because it was the toneless voice of an idiot.

Dominick Vane tigged at the revolver in the holster under his arm. The whole world was whirling around him now, but somehow he knew that he must get out that gun or he and Jaxon would face the same fate that Ted Drewes had met. The roar of the revolver was the last thing Vane remembered.

CHAPTER IV

WALL STREET

DOMINICK VANE OPENED his eyes. It was daylight. He was lying between cool white sheets of a very comfortable bed. A streak of morning sunlight stretched across the soft gray of the ceiling. For a moment or two Vane could not seem to collect his thoughts—could not remember where he was or how he had gotten there. He turned his head slowly on the pillow. Then he remembered that nightmare of the pine barrens, and he wondered if it was not in reality just that—a bad dream.

"How do you feel, old man?"

Vane turned quickly to see Philip Jaxon standing beside the bed, dressed in a handsome silk robe, looking down at him with a wry smile. Then Vane remembered that last moment of consciousness: the white-haired creature on the bank of the pool pointing the extinguisher at Jaxon.

"We're at my place," said Jaxon, seeing bewilderment in the agent's eyes. "We had a close squeak, if you ask me."

"How did we get here?" Vane asked, struggling to recall something beyond that moment in the pool of water.

"Carried you most of the way on my back," said Jaxon casually, "until we got close enough to home for me to yowl for help."

Vane sat up in bed and ran his fingers nervously through his hair. "I'm not dreaming, am I, Jaxon? We did see marching men in gas masks? We did nearly pass out as a result of inhaling the stuff? We did run into Hardwick's white-haired monster?"

"We did," said Jaxon grimly. "And if you hadn't shot him I doubt very much if we'd be talking about it now."

"I shot him?"

"You emptied your gun into his chest," said Jaxon quietly. He took a cigarette from the pocket of his silk robe and lit it. "Then you passed out." He looked down at his fingernails. "I had the foresight to bring that little brass tube along with me, Vane. I squirted a drop or two of its contents on a piece of cloth in the kitchen. It eats through cloth and wood like fire. It's plenty bad stuff… and Furno was about to let go with a charge of it full into my face. You saved my life."

"And you mine," said Vane.

"Let's forget that part of it," said Jaxon. He sat down on the edge of the bed and looked into Vane's haggard face. "What does it all mean, Dominick?" he asked. "What's going on out there? What were those men drilling for?"

"I don't know," said Vane. He passed a hand over his eyes, which were still sore and red from the encounter with the gas the night before. "I only got a moment's look at them before I realized we had to get out of there. They were armed with rifles."

"Right. And there were little crimson bands around the sleeves of the gray shirts they wore. Those men weren't pineys, Dominick."

"But the man you called Furno?" Vane asked.

"One of the pineys I knew," said Jaxon. "Where he got hold of that little brass toy of his I don't know."

"From our friends with the rifles, the artillery, the gas masks and the gas," said Vane. He swung his feet over the side of the bed. "Look here, Philip, how many people know what happened to us last night?"

"Only Angela knows the real truth," said Jaxon. "She was waiting when we got back. I had to tell her, but she'll be silent as a clam. She promised not to say a word to anyone until you came to and decided on a course of action. The servants simply think we had an accident of some sort."

"Good," said Dominick Vane. His strength was slowly coming back to him. "I must get in touch with Washington at once. Then we'll decide what to do."

"I'll have the butler plug a phone in here for you," said Jaxon. "You'll be able to talk in complete privacy that way." As he finished speaking there came a discreet knock at the door. "Well?"

"It's Devins, sir." The door opened to disclose the butler. "Your uncle, Mr. Dawson, and a friend are here, sir. They—"

BUT BEFORE the butler could finish a man brushed past him and came into the room. H.R. Dawson was almost as familiar a figure in America as the President. Everyone knew this suave, elegant man of fifty-five, said to be the greatest financial power in the country. He was immaculate in a short black coat and striped gray trousers. He wore a gray silk cravat against his wing collar, ornamented by a handsome black pearl stick-pin. The waxed gray mustache and sleek gray hair completed a picture of rich sartorial dignity.

"Philip, my boy, I couldn't wait to be announced," he said. "I was terribly anxious about you."

"Anxious, uncle?"

"After your experience of last night, of course!" H.R. Dawson's voice had just the proper note of concern in it. "This gentleman is, I presume, Mr. Vane? Thank God you are both quite all right."

Jaxon was about to reply when another man came into the room. A fat man in a plain business suit. He wore a soft-brimmed black hat pulled down over squinting little black eyes that were sunk in pouchy sockets. He was a big man, broad of shoulder, huge of girth, and yet he walked with an almost catlike tread. He had flabby, sensuous lips which he kept moistening with the tip of his tongue. His shirt was none too clean, and there were food stains on the rather gaudy purple tie he wore.

"Ah, Moxelli," said H.R. Dawson, "this is my nephew, Philip Jaxon, and his friend, Mr. Vane. Moxelli is a business associate of mine, Philip."

The thick lips of Moxelli twisted into a curious little one-sided smile. "I am delighted to meet you both," he said. His voice was soft, almost a whisper. The little pig eyes looked only at Dominick Vane, who still sat on the edge of his bed. "You had quite a time, by all accounts."

"Look here, uncle, how the devil did you know anything about last night?" Jaxon asked sharply.

"Why—Angela told me, of course," said Dawson smoothly.

"I'm rather surprised," said Jaxon. "Because she promised me to say nothing to anyone."

"You could hardly expect her to keep it from me, her father, Philip," said H.R. Dawson. "Moxelli happened to be at the house at the time and we were both very much concerned about you. For heaven's sake tell us exactly what happened."

Dominick Vane spoke for the first time. "Perhaps Miss Dawson also told you that I am a government agent, Mr. Dawson. I am very anxious that nothing of our experience should be known until we've had a chance to investigate further."

Moxelli smiled that one-sided little smile. "Is there more to know than that you found men drilling in the middle of the pine barrens, that you were nearly badly gassed, and that you had to kill a man to keep him from emptying a container of acid in your faces?" he asked softly.

Vane's cold blue eyes were fixed on the fat man's face. "You seem to be thoroughly informed," he said. "I can only ask that you keep this entirely to yourselves until such time as we see fit to break the story."

"Anything you say, of course," said H.R. Dawson hastily. "But I am gravely concerned for my nephew's safety. Of course it is too late to criticize your judgment, Mr. Vane, in taking him on this expedition with you. But now that it has been done I am wondering as to what his best course of action would be. You are quite obviously up against some sort of very sinister business. Philip knows so much his life may be in danger. I came here to suggest that he leave Marshfield at once until the government forces have cleared up this business."

"My judgment may have been faulty," said Vane coldly, "but it so happens your nephew saved my life."

"My dear sir," said H.R. Dawson, "I am not questioning Philip's courage. I simply think he should get as far away from this mess as he can until it is cleared up. Come down to my place on Long Island, Philip, and stay there until this thing has blown over."

"I rather think I'll stay here and string along with Vane if he'll have me," said Philip.

"That would be a mistake," said Moxelli, very softly indeed.

For a moment no one spoke. Somehow the whole atmosphere seemed to be electrically charged. Dawson tugged nervously at one of the waxed ends of his mustache. Moxelli only smiled that one-sided smile, and licked his lips. His eyes never left Dominick Vane's face, as if he were fascinated by the government man.

"If you don't mind, uncle," said Philip Jaxon, "I think I'll talk this over with Vane. We've been in this together up to now. If he thinks it's advisable for me to leave Marshfield, I'll let you know."

There was a silence, as shrill—somehow—as the sharpest of noises. Uncle and nephew surveyed each other coolly, questioning, appraising, deciding.

H.R. Dawson shrugged his elegant shoulders. "I cannot force you to follow my advice, Philip. All I can say is that I think it would be criminally foolish for you to lift another finger in this affair."

"Better do what your uncle says," said Moxelli.

"I'm very grateful to you for your interest in my safety, Mr. Moxelli," said Jaxon coldly, "but I must ask you to allow me to make my own decisions."

Moxelli moistened his thick lips. "It's your funeral," he said. Almost reluctantly, it seemed, he looked away from Dominick Vane to Dawson. "We'd better be getting right along," he said.

Dawson nodded. "I can only urge you earnestly to consider my suggestion, Philip. Goodbye. Goodbye, Mr. Vane."

Alone, Jaxon and Vane looked at one another in silence for a moment.

"Queer sort of business associate, that fellow Moxelli," said Jaxon.

"Very queer indeed," said Dominick Vane. "The man was a walking arsenal, Philip. Gun under each arm—and the eyes of a killer if I ever saw them."

CHAPTER V

EXTERMINATION

CONSULTATION WITH CORCORAN in Washington brought about some very quick action. A little more than an hour later, under Vane's leadership, a body of State Police augmented by about fifteen G-men who were rushed from Washington by plane, began an excursion into the barrens. Armed to the teeth, this force was, with rifles, rapid-fire guns, grenades, and gas masks. It was a trail of death they followed, for as they approached the clearing, where the night before Vane and Jaxon had seen the masked men drilling, they found the barrens littered with the dead bodies of animals and birds; a fox or two, woodchucks, squirrels, birds of all kinds, and even the bony carcass of a mongrel dog.

Vane had been leading the way with a G-man named Morse, who had worked with him before, at his elbow. "Looks as though you and your friend Jaxon got out of here just in time last night. That gas must have been bad stuff."

Vane looked puzzled. "I wonder, Roy. Or was this something else that was turned loose later?" He felt a cold chill run along his spine. "The piney village lies just ahead, according to Jaxon. You don't suppose…" He didn't finish, but he quickened his stride, that diamond-hard light glittering in his eyes. Somehow he knew what they were going to find, yet the idea was so horrible that he refused to accept it.

They found the great open space where the men had drilled, the burnt-out torches still stuck in the ground. Beyond were the shacks of the piney village, yet there was no sign of life there now. No one appeared to greet them as they moved swiftly forward, weapons drawn, ready for any sort of surprise attack that might await them. But no attack came.

Outside the first shack they reached lay another dead dog, his nose pressed against the rickety door as if he had been trying to get in when he died. Gun in hand Dominick Vane kicked open the door of the shack and went in.

"Mother of—!" It was a hoarse whisper from Morse at Vane's elbow.

There were five dead people in the shack, a man, a woman, and three children. The man was an albino, as were the three children. There were no wounds of any sort on the bodies.

"Some kind of lethal gas," said Dominick Vane grimly.

They went on, and in every shack of that miserable little community they found the owners dead. Not a single person out of more than fifty had escaped, not an animal for a distance of nearly a mile in all directions had survived. Everywhere was complete destruction of life in every form. The pineys had been harboring some outside force, that was clear, but with the danger of discovery imminent that force had brutally wiped out those wretched people who had sheltered them. Not a living soul remained to tell these officers of the law what had been going on out here in the silence of the woods.

Nor was there any trace of the armament that Vane knew must have existed—no trace of the guns that had pitted the woods with shell holes—no trace of the rifles with which that sinister force had been drilling. Later they found the body of Furno, lying by the little pool where Vane had shot him. The destruction of that village was complete.

PHILIP JAXON had not accompanied Vane on this expedition. The G-men had received orders from Washington, strict orders to exclude him. Corcoran had explained it on a routine basis, but something in his voice had puzzled Vane. He wondered if by any chance H.R. Dawson had already used his influence to make certain his nephew had no part in things.

But Jaxon, champing, restless on the bit at home, was not to have an entirely eventless morning. Just a little before noon Devins came out onto the terrace with a card on a little silver tray. Jaxon looked at it.

Mr. Samuel Seaver
Real Estate

Ordinarily Jaxon might not have seen him, but this morning anything was better than inaction.

"Show him out here, Devins," he said.

Jaxon took an instinctive dislike to Mr. Samuel Seaver. He was a slim young man with black hair brushed slickly back from a very low forehead, and there was a curious, almost Oriental slant to his black eyes. He smiled a very white-toothed smile and held out an unpleasantly moist hand to the young sportsman.

"What can I do for you, Mr. Seaver?" Philip asked, without enthusiasm.

Mr. Seaver pulled one of the wicker chairs close to Philip and sat down. "I've got a wonderful proposition for you, Mr. Jaxon— a really wonderful proposition." He rubbed his hands together as though the thought of it was excessively pleasant to him. "I've got a client. He wants to rent your house for the summer."

"My house is not for rent," said Philip coldly.

Seaver laughed. "But there is a price for everything, eh, Mr. Jaxon. My client has been all over Jersey, all over Long Island, all over Westchester, and yours is the only place he has seen that he wants. He is prepared to offer you ten thousand dollars for your place from now till October."

"I have already told you the place is not for rent," said Jaxon.

"Fifteen thousand! How about fifteen thousand, Mr. Jaxon?"

"Nothing doing," said Philip, with finality.

Mr. Seaver looked distressed. "You must know how it is with

a very rich man, Mr. Jaxon. When he wants something he wants it. Price is no object. Suppose you say what you would rent it for."

"I wouldn't rent it for anything, Mr. Seaver. I built the place because I like it myself, and I want to live here myself, and I'm not renting. Who is this client of yours anyhow?"

"I'm not at liberty to say," said Mr. Seaver.

Philip was suddenly very angry. He believed along with Vane that he had been excluded from that expedition into the barrens because of his uncle's influence. Now he suspected that this was another move of Dawson's to get him away from Marshfield.

Again Philip faced a man, questioning, testing, deciding.

"Tell your client," he said grimly, "that nothing on earth would persuade me to give up the place; that I expect to live here all summer myself. There is nothing more to be said about it, Mr. Seaver."

Seaver shrugged. "You might be sorry," he said.

Philip got up so abruptly from his chair that it fell over backwards on the flagstone terrace. "Get out!" he rapped.

IT WAS late afternoon before Dominick Vane returned to the Jaxon house. He had made a report to Washington of the discovery of the Village of the Dead. Corcoran had ordered him to stay on the scene for a few hours more unless, at his own judgment, something should turn up that would justify his leaving. Telegraph wires were clicking to all parts of the country to manufacturers of arms. Who had supplied hundreds of rifles to a secret organization? Who had equipped them with gas masks? What chemical plant had produced a lethal gas which had wiped out a whole village in the course of a night and laid waste to the fauna of the countryside? Military and Naval intelligence operatives were on the job as well as the G-men. Vane had sent the brass tube of acid, which the albino Furno had dropped, to a famous laboratory in New York. First reports were that the acid was an unknown product to them. It would take time to make an analysis of it.

Somehow, after the terrible day, Philip's story of the visit of Samuel Seaver seemed a little tame to Vane.

"Your uncle seems determined to get you out of here, Philip," he said.

Philip had offered, in fact had insisted, that Vane stay at the Marshfield house along with Roy Morse, the other G-man. Morse sat most of the night at the telephone picking up reports from the Department in Washington, trying to piece them together into a picture that made sense. Dominick Vane slept. He was close to exhaustion. After midnight Morse curled up on a couch in the living room, close to the phone. There was no definite information of any kind. Every arms manufacturer in the country denied the sale of rifles, machine guns, field pieces, gas masks, or any other equipment to any organization unlicensed by the government. No chemical plant would admit the sale of gas, or the manufacture of an acid like that in Furno's brass tube. It was a very blank wall they found themselves against.

And then about five-thirty in the morning the Jaxon household was thrown into an uproar. Morse was wakened by a hysterical pounding on the front door which quickly roused everyone else. Jaxon, Vane, Devins, all came running. The front door was thrown open to disclose Ryan, Jaxon's head groom in a state bordering on collapse.

"Please, sir, come down to the stables at once."

A ghastly spectacle awaited them. Six fine hunters and four crack polo ponies lay dead in their stalls. Two spotted Dalmatian coach dogs were stretched out on the floor. And upstairs, in a loft room, the body of a stable boy was crumpled near the door he had tried to open in an effort at escape.

Philip stood leaning against an upright beam, dazed, unashamed tears running down his cheeks. The stable boy had been a faithful servant. He had loved these animals. Morse, Devins and the groom seemed as stunned as the stricken young owner. Only Dominick Vane retained anything of balance. He examined the body of the stable boy.

"The same thing we encountered in the barrens," he said grimly, "—gas." He turned on Ryan, the groom. "What time were the stables closed?"

"About ten o'clock, sir. That was when Jerry and I turned in. Jerry was a fine lad, sir."

"Not a sniff of anything in the air now," said Dominick Vane. "They must have gone to work shortly after you shut up shop." He paused abruptly, his eyes on the inside of the big stable doors. "Look," he said harshly.

Scrawled across the door in big crimson letters was a message:

JAXON!
GET OUT UNLESS YOU WANT SOME OF THIS.

Philip Jaxon cried: "We've got to find them, Vane! *We've got to find them!*"

Dominick's face was white and tense. "I think we may have been doing your uncle an injustice, Philip," he said. "He wouldn't turn his hand to anything like this to get you out of here." Then he pounded his clenched fist into the palm of the other hand. "Seaver!" he cried. "Did you save that card, Philip? Was there an address on it?"

CHAPTER VI

INFORMER

MR. SAMUEL SEAVER slept. It was seven o'clock in the morning and since Mr. Seaver had only turned in about two hours before that and since he had been quite drunk when he turned in, he slept very hard. It was a barren little room on the top floor of a brownstone house in the West Forties that he occupied, furnished only with a bed, a table, and a couple of chairs. Cigarette stubs littered the table and the uncarpeted floor. Mr. Seaver's rather fancy Broadway clothes were strewn unceremoniously about. Mr. Seaver slept so soundly that he did not hear the sharp knock at his door. But he was rudely and startlingly awakened when the door was suddenly burst open by a man's stout shoulder. Mr. Seaver sat up in bed and saw that he had three visitors.

"Say, what the hell…" said Mr. Seaver, angrily And then he saw the haggard face of Philip Jaxon, and some of his assurance left him. Nor did Mr. Seaver like the way one of the other men quietly closed the door and leaned against it. Nor did he like the cold, hard glitter in the eyes of the third man who came slowly over toward the bed.

"So these are the real-estate offices of Samuel Seaver," said Dominick Vane grimly.

"You got me wrong," said Seaver. "This isn't my office."

"Ah, so you *have* an office?" Vane's voice was dangerously soft.

Seaver squirmed a little. "Well, you see, as a matter of fact I'm sort of a contact man. Sort of a promotion man. Get it?"

"No," said Dominick Vane.

"Well, I don't work from an office. I just go around meeting them and—"

"Who was the client you told Mr. Jaxon wanted to rent his house?" Vane cut in.

Seaver squirmed some more. "I'm not at liberty to say. You know how that is, don't you? I simply—"

Dominick Vane's right hand shot out, caught Seaver by the back of the neck and wrenched him out of the bed into the middle of the floor, shivering. "There's been murder done in the last twenty-four hours, Seaver," he said harshly. "Mass murder of the most horrible sort. You know about it. Start talking quickly if you ever want to walk out of this room whole."

Roy Morse, the other federal agent, had come over from the door. Seaver, quaking with fear, found himself surrounded by three men who looked grim as death.

"You can't do this to me," he whined. "I got rights. I'm a citizen. I'll have the law on you."

Morse hit him squarely in the middle of the mouth and he fell, blubbering to his knees. Vane yanked him up to his feet again.

"I'm giving you a chance, Seaver," said Vane steadily. "Who were you representing when you called at Marshfield today? What do you know about the foul business that happened out there tonight? What do you know about those men who have been using the pine barrens out there as a drill ground… who wiped out a whole village last night with poison gas?"

"I tell you I don't know," said Seaver.

Morse hit him again, a jolting blow on the point of the jaw that sent him smashing back against the iron frame of the bed. "Talk, sweetheart, and talk in a hurry," said Morse.

"Who sent you to Marshfield to see Philip Jaxon?" Vane demanded.

Seaver looked around him like a hunted animal, licking his

bleeding lips. "You know what would happen to me if I did any talking," he said.

"So it wasn't a client?"

"Well, not exactly," said Seaver. "There's a fellow named Lefty Brace I've done some jobs for. He said *he* had a client, and would I go out to Marshfield and—"

"Never mind the hooey," said Morse grimly. "Who is Lefty Brace?"

"He's a fellow around town. A sort of a—"

MORSE GRABBED Seaver's arm about the wrist and clamped it next to his body. He grabbed Seaver's little finger and bent it back sharply. "I'll break this and every other finger on both your hands if you don't start giving us the straight dope," he said.

"You can't do that," Seaver screamed. "Ever if you're a cop you can't do that. I'll have you kicked off the force. I'll—"

"Brother, when we get through with you," said Morse, "if you haven't done some mighty glib talking, we'll just put what's left of you in the waste basket. Now. Who is Lefty Brace? And if you don't come clean I'm through kidding!"

Seaver struggled for a moment to free himself from the painful grip in which Morse held him. Then he stopped, panting for breath, sweat running off his face. Obviously he was afraid to talk, but his fear of these three grim-faced men was greater.

"I'll tell you who Brace is," he said finally, "only let up on my finger." Morse relaxed his grip slightly. Seaver gulped in his breath. "He's one of the big shots in the Red Sleeves."

"The Red Sleeves?" Vane's voice was sharp. Those drilling men in the pine barrens had worn little scarlet bands on the arms of their gray shirts.

Words literally bubbled out of Seaver now that he had begun to talk. "Sure. You must of heard of the Red Sleeves! There's thousands of 'em all over the country… North, East, West and South. There's hundreds of training grounds like that one out in the barrens where they teach 'em military tactics, how to handle guns, and grenades, street fighting— the works. Lefty calls 'em 'murder farms.' They're gettin' ready for a big blow-off. It may come any day now, and when it does, it'll be too bad for the ones in power now."

"Revolution?" asked Dominick Vane.

"What else?" asked Seaver with a shrug.

"Who's back of it? Communists... Fascists...?"

"Search me," said Seaver. "I only know Lefty. But there's dough back of it. These guys have got the best in equipment and plenty of it. I don't know anything more than I'm tellin' you. I don't know anyone in it but Lefty. Maybe he ain't one of the big shots, but he's the only one I know."

"Where can we find Lefty Brace?"

"You wouldn't ask me to go that far!" Seaver cried. "These fellows won't stop at nothin'! They...."

"We know," said Dominick Vane grimly. "Where's Lefty Brace?"

"Come clean," said Morse, and increased the pressure of his grip on Seaver's finger.

Seaver began to cry. "This means the works for me," he said. "They'll get me. They...."

"They won't get you, my friend," said Vane coldly, "because you're going to be safely hidden away in jail."

"No place is going to be safe when the Red Sleeves get going," said Seaver desperately. "They've got men in the jails... men ready to let out the most desperate killers. They've got men in the banks, in the railroads, at the airports, on the ships. They've got men everywhere, I tell you. Even in the Army and Navy. In all the big plants and factories, in the radio stations. I tell you, mister, these guys mean business. And anyone who plays 'em dirt...."

"I'm asking you for the last time," said Dominick Vane quietly, "where's this Lefty Brace?"

Seaver sighed. It was like the deflation of a balloon. He seemed to shrivel and grow smaller. "Okay," he said, in an odd cracked voice. "Maybe it don't make so much difference. Maybe in a few days none of us won't be around anyhow. When they start dropping gas bombs on this man's town people are going to be dropping in the streets like flies. You'll find Lefty Brace in the Hotel Mordaunt and for your sake I hope he don't get wise you're coming. Because he'd shoot you as soon as eat his breakfast. There ain't any of the Red Sleeves worrying very much about law and order right now. Because in a few days—"

"Get on some clothes," said Dominick Vane. "You're going with us."

FIVE MINUTES later this little group of four men emerged from the brownstone house. Seaver and Morse were walking first, arm in arm, as though they were pals. Dominick Vane walked behind, the gun in his coat pocket covering Seaver.

Even afterward Dominick Vane did not know what had warned him of danger. All he knew was that he looked suddenly up the street and saw a curtained touring car bearing down on them at a terrific rate of speed.

"Roy!" he shouted at Morse. "Duck for cover." At the same instant he turned and literally hurled Philip Jaxon into the alley between the house from which they had just emerged and the next. He came plunging after and both of them fell in a heap behind a couple of metal ash cans. At the same moment the staccato rattle of a machine gun split the morning air. Dominick Vane caught a glimpse of the car as he lay on his belly in the dirt. He saw the gun spouting flame… saw Roy Morse and the unfortunate Mr. Seaver riddled by its bullets. And he saw more than that. He saw the face of the machine-gunner. A fat face with flabby lips that were twisted into a cruel, one-sided smile.

"Moxelli!" Dominick Vane emptied his gun hopelessly after the flying car.

Then for a moment Dominick Vane leaned against the brick wall of the alley in which he and Philip had taken cover, fighting back the wave of nausea that swept over him. The sight of that curtained car—the rattle of the machine gun—brought rocketing back into his memory that terrible day five years before when he had held the dead body of the woman he loved in his arms.

It was Jaxon who brought him back to earth; Jaxon who asked in a shaken voice: "Dominick, are you all right? You're not hit?"

Vane's teeth clamped tightly together. "I'm all right," he said. "God help Morse and Seaver!"

People were running from everywhere now, including a couple of cops who came puffing up from Broadway to the spot where Morse and Seaver lay in a pool of crimson on the pavement. Dominick Vane went out of the alley, smoking gun still in his hands, and was almost shot for his pains by an over-zealous officer who thought he was one of the participants in a pistol duel. Vane showed his credentials and explained briefly what had happened. The morgue wagon was sent for and before it arrived Vane took Philip by the arm and led him down the street. The young millionaire looked as though he were about to cave in. Sudden and violent death of this sort was a new experience to him.

"Did you notice," he whispered to Vane, "Morse's fingers… he was gripping Seaver's wrist so tightly, even in death, they had to pry them loose. Dominick, who are these murderers? Why… why this wholesale slaughter?"

Vane steered the young man into a restaurant. "A bottle of brandy and two glasses," he said to the wide eyed proprietor.

"I'm sorry, sir. Our bar isn't open till—"

"Open it!" rapped Vane, "and be quick about it!"

When Dominick Vane gave orders people obeyed them. The manager returned in a moment with a bottle of Courvoisier and two glasses. His hands shook a little as he put them down on the table.

"Those other two…" he said hesitantly. "They're dead?"

"What do *you* think?" Vane said sharply.

The manager filled the two glasses with brandy and went away, leaving the bottle.

"I… I don't think I can take it, Dominick," said Philip.

"Drink it!" said Vane sharply. He tossed off his own and refilled the glass.

PHILIP, AFTER a little shudder, drank and then permitted Vane to refill his glass. "You could drink a pint of this now and not feel it," said Vane. He lit a cigarette and inhaled deeply on it for a moment or two in silence. Then he turned to Philip and that diamond-hard light glittered in his cold blue eyes.

"Philip, did you see the murder car?" he asked.

"Just a glimpse," said Philip. "I… I was too busy taking cover behind those ash cans."

"I saw more than that," said Vane. "I got a good look at the machine-gunner." He blew a cloud of smoke toward the ceiling. "It was Moxelli!"

"*What!*" Philip was incredulous.

"No doubt whatever about it," said Dominick Vane.

"But...."

"Listen," said Vane grimly. "I don't know what it means any more than you do. Your uncle may know him in a quite innocent capacity. The fact remains that Moxelli himself is all tied up in this mess. He knew plenty when he visited us in Marshfield yesterday. More than that, Philip, do you realize that we must have been followed, else how would they have been ready for us when we came out of Seaver's? They guessed Seaver would talk and they wanted to do for us before we made a report on our conversation."

Philip tossed off his second brandy. "Then you think all that talk of Seaver's about revolution—about the Red Sleeves—was on the level? It sounded like a fairy story to me."

Dominick Vane's laugh was short and mirthless. "Was there anything unreal about those dead pineys, or the massacre in your stable, or that murder car? Would they go in for this wholesale killing unless there was something tremendous at stake?"

Philip's hand shook as he lifted the brandy glass to his lips. "You're right, of course," he said. "What—what happens now?"

"If Seaver was telling us the whole truth," said Dominick Vane, "we've got to work with lightning speed, Philip. If the Red Sleeves are as big and powerful an organization as he says it may already be too late. But do you remember one thing he said? That there was big money back of them. You don't have to be very bright to jump to a conclusion, Philip—a damned unpleasant conclusion for you. Moxelli is one of them, and Moxelli is your uncle's friend, and your uncle is lousy with money!"

"It doesn't seem credible," said Philip. "And yet...."

"I want you to go to your uncle at once," said Dominick Vane. "I want you to question him as adroitly and cleverly as you can.

I want you to find out as much as possible without letting him know just how much *you* know. Are you game?"

"Of course. He won't talk if he *is* involved, though."

"But you'll be able to come to a pretty definite conclusion about him," Vane said.

"Right. And you?" Philip asked.

"I'm making a report to Washington at once," said Vane. Then his lips tightened. "Then I'm going on to the Hotel Mordaunt to see Mr. Lefty Brace."

"Alone?"

"Alone," said Dominick Vane. He looked searchingly at the younger man. "Philip, I think we're up to our ears in something big. We know how cheaply life is held in this game. If you want to get out of it now… get! Take the first boat for Europe and stay away until it's over. There's no reason why you—"

"Don't be silly," said Philip, smiling very faintly. "You know I have no intention of getting out."

"Yes, I guess I know it," said Dominick Vane softly. He lit a fresh cigarette. "Your uncle is at his town house?"

"As far as I know."

"Good. Go and see Dawson at once. I'll meet you at the University Club in exactly two hours."

"Right," said Philip, as Vane rose from the table. "See you later, and good hunting, Dominick!"

"Thanks," said Vane.

CHAPTER VII

AVUNCULAR PLAN

DOMINICK VANE FLASHED his credentials on the pasty-faced clerk who stood behind the desk at the Hotel Mordaunt.

"I'm looking for a man named Brace," he said shortly. "I want his room number."

If he was surprised, nothing in the clerk's face showed it. "Room 1511," he said laconically. "Shall I announce you?"

Vane's lips were tight set. "I suppose you will anyhow the minute I start for the elevator," he said. "You can tell Brace I'm on my way up." He turned and went to the elevator. Five minutes later he was knocking on the door of Room 1511. He waited, his right hand sunk in the pocket of his coat and closed over the butt of his gun. There was only a moment's delay before the door opened to reveal Lefty Brace.

Brace was short, stocky, red-haired, with the quick, shifting eyes of a fighter. Somehow Vane knew that in the first flash of their meeting Brace had made a quick and accurate estimate of his visitor.

"Hello, copper," he said in a husky voice.

"Mind if I come in?" Vane asked dryly. He was already across the threshold of the room. He saw that Brace, too, was prepared. He was wearing a long, silk dressing-gown and his hands were sunk in the pockets. The right one bulged suspiciously.

"Why not?" said Brace, and closed the door. He moved quickly, alertly, managing always to keep Vane in front of him.

"To what am I indebted for the honor of this visit, as they say in the movies?"

"Know a man named Samuel Seaver?" Vane asked abruptly.

"No," said Brace, promptly. He took a cigarette from the left pocket of his dressing gown, put it between his lips, and then struck a match with his thumb nail. "Should I know Mr. Samuel Seaver, copper?" Lefty Brace's eyes never left Vane's face for an instant.

"It wouldn't be a valuable friendship now," said Vane. "Seaver is dead. Shot to death in front of his house about an hour ago."

"Maybe you want me to bust out crying," said Brace. "But since I didn't know the man—"

"He was on his way to bring me here to see you, Brace. He seemed to know you all right."

Brace shrugged. "A lot of people know me," he said. "Up and down Broadway and at the race tracks. I'm what the columnists call a character, copper. What was this Seaver, a tout? Give you a bum steer?"

"I don't think so," said Dominick Vane. "Did you read the papers this morning about the massacre of a village of pineys out in Marshfield, New Jersey?"

"Yeah. Damn funny business," said Brace. The cigarette bobbed up and down between his lips as he talked.

"Seaver seemed to think you might know all about it," said Vane coolly. "He seemed to think you might know who murdered Philip Jaxon's stable boy last night and killed about a dozen valuable animals."

"This Seaver was screwy," said Brace.

"By the way, where were you last night from, say, ten until five-thirty this morning?"

Brace laughed. "Think I was out in Marshfield bumping off horses?"

Vane's cold eyes had a dangerous glitter in them. "Who said anything about horses, Lefty?"

Brace didn't bat an eye, but Vane saw the hand in the dressing-gown pocket contract dangerously. "Why, you did, copper."

"I said animals. I didn't say horses."

Brace smiled a tight-lipped smile. "Funny. I could have sworn you said horses. And anyhow, I couldn't have been in Marshfield, because I was down in Greenwich Village killing another guy." He laughed. "An old cobbler who forgot to put rubber heels on a pair of shoes I took in to have repaired. I'm very particular about heels."

Vane was silent for a moment. Finally he asked, in a casual tone. "Ever hear of the Red Sleeves, Brace?"

"Let's see," said Brace, adopting an elaborate air of thoughtfulness. "I got it! They sell Christmas seals!"

"Wrong," said Vane grimly.

"Funny. I was sure they sold Christmas seals. Red Sleeves! Of course I know the Red *Sox;* they're a Boston baseball club. Then there are the Redmen; that's a slang phrase for the American Indian. But Red Sleeves! I guess you got me there, copper. I give up. Who *are* the Red Sleeves?"

"They're a revolutionary organization that goes in for murder in a big way," said Dominick Vane, slowly. "I understand you're one of the big shots in the organization."

"If I am they must have made me an honorary colonel without my knowing it," said Brace. "They did that to me down in Kentucky once. Derby Week, you know. But then I never cared much for honor and glory—if you see what I mean."

Dominick Vane looked at Brace steadily for a moment. "Brace," he said quietly. "I understand the lid is coming off any day now. When and if it does, you're one guy we'll come straight after. You might save yourself a lot of grief by spilling the beans now. We won't handle you with kid gloves if you haven't helped us."

Brace's eyes glinted dangerously. "It's been fun knowing you, copper," he said dryly, "but I suddenly find myself fed up with you and your line. Suppose we cut this short—unless of course you have some evidence against me that would justify your making an arrest."

Dominick Vane sighed. "I haven't any evidence against you, Brace. Only the testimony of a man who, very conveniently for you, is dead. I had hoped you might do a little talking, but since you won't you're just making it harder for yourself and for us. We'll get evidence against you, Brace, because you're in this up to your ears. And when we do we may not bother to make an arrest."

"Killed while resisting arrest, eh?"

"Something like that," said Dominick Vane. "And I hope I'm the one you resist, Lefty. You see, I'm very particular about heels myself!"

Color flared up into Brace's cheeks. "Get out!" he snapped.

"Be seeing you," said Dominick Vane softly.

THE BUTLER at the town house of H.R. Dawson permitted himself a smile as he opened the door for Philip Jaxon.

"Glad to see you, Mr. Philip."

"Thanks, Remsen. Is my uncle here, or has he gone to the office?"

"He's in his study, sir. I'll tell him you're here."

"Never mind, Remsen, I'll announce myself," said Philip. He caught a glimpse of himself in the hall mirror as he turned toward the study door and was shocked at his appearance. He was very pale and there were deep hollows under his eyes. He paused for a second outside the study, and then, without knocking, let himself in.

H.R. Dawson sat at a big flat-topped desk in the center of the room. He was immaculate as usual in a gray worsted suit, wing collar, and a polka-dot bow tie. He was looking at some papers and a pair of pince nez, attached to a black cord he wore around his neck, were perched on the end of his nose. As Philip entered he looked up.

If there had been any doubts in Philip's mind as to the possibility of Vane's suggestion that Dawson had some hand in this whole terrible affair they were dispelled at that moment. The glasses dropped from Dawson's nose and his lips parted. Slowly every vestige of color drained from his face, leaving it the color and texture of old parchment.

"Philip!" It was an almost inaudible whisper.

"Yes, I am here, uncle," said Philip grimly. His hands were clenched very tightly at his sides. "No thanks to you, however."

"Why—why what do you mean, Philip?"

"You didn't expect to see me, did you, uncle?" Philip asked bitterly. "You didn't ever expect to see me again, did you?" Suddenly Dominick Vane's warning against showing his hand too openly disappeared into thin air as the tension of the last twenty-four hours suddenly smashed his control of himself. "You damned slimy murderer!"

"Philip!"

Philip laughed, a little wildly. "Worried about me, were you? Rushed out to Marshfield because Angela told you what had happened! You and your murdering side-kick Moxelli knew what had happened all right—but you didn't know it from Angela! You knew it from your hoodlums and killers! You turned them loose in my stable because you wanted me to get away from Marshfield—thought I might find out too much! Then you turned them loose on me and on Vane with a machine gun—tried to mow us down in the streets like rats!"

"Wait, Philip… *listen!*" Dawson interrupted sharply. "I wanted to get you away from there to save you. I—"

"Then you don't deny it!"

Very slowly Dawson raised a hand to his carefully waxed mustache. "No, I don't deny it, Philip."

"What the hell are you trying to do?" Philip stormed. "Who are these murdering Red Sleeves you're financing? Revolutionists, Seaver said. What have you to do with revolutions? What have you to do with this wholesale killing? Have you lost your mind?"

"Listen, Philip... You've got to *listen!*" Dawson said His voice was suddenly hard, his gray eyes impelling. "I would have told you all this sooner or later, but up to now I haven't been at liberty to do so. This unfortunate affair in Marshfield has forced everything into the open much sooner than I expected. I don't deny my association with the Red Sleeves. They're powerful, Philip. More powerful than you dream. Hundreds of thousands of them all over the country, thoroughly equipped and prepared, ready and waiting for the signal."

"Signal for what?" demanded Philip.

"Revolution," said Dawson softly. "The time has come, Philip, to cast off the yoke of a corrupt political machine, to crush out a tyranny of petty politicians, to give America back to the Americans!"

"Bunk! Soap-box oratory! What are you driving at?"

"Philip—have you been so absorbed with your horses and your social life that you have failed to see this country careening toward chaos? We used to call it 'Depression' a few years ago. And we are supposed to have come out of it now—but we've not, Philip. Thousands are still starving, millions are existing only by government subsidy. No man knows what lies ahead. Philip, the mass mind is no longer competent to rule America; our bulky, awkward party system is tottering. Strikes—long bloody industrial sieges—are tearing great holes in our industry. The mass mind will not stop them; we have waited too long for people to act at the polls. To save America from sliding into chaos and anarchy with the rest of the world, we must act now—and by force!"

PHILIP STARED at his uncle. "And where does H.R. Dawson fit into this picture?"

Dawson tugged at his mustache. "I have made my money out of America, my boy," he said. "I'm prepared to spend that money to help America back on its feet."

"Well, I'm damned!" said Philip softly. "Do you think for one minute I'll swallow that line, uncle? Who writes your speeches for you? Moxelli, your fat-faced killer? Or was it the oily Mr. Seaver—who got himself shot? Or Lefty Brace? Uncle, you have made your fortune by crushing the weak, by stepping on the neck of everybody who got in your way. You have gypped the government on oil leases, you have dealt out more economic misery in your day than any other man in the country. What *is* all this patriotic hooey from you? I know damned well that if you are backing this revolutionary movement it is because there is some gain in it for you. What do you get out of it, uncle? Are you going to be the American Hitler? Are you going to be king?"

"Philip, you're unstrung," said Dawson quietly. "You've been through a terrible experience in the last few hours. I would have saved you from it if I could. But when you understand what's behind this you'll find yourself fighting shoulder to shoulder with us. You doubt my motives in this, but in a few days the whole country will know my motives and applaud them."

"You're darn right they'll know them," Philip cried. "They'll know them before a few days. I'm going to shout them from the house-tops! The leopard can't change his spots, and a Dawson never does anything that isn't strictly for personal gain. The public is going to know that these fine-sounding speeches of yours are boloney! They're going to know it from *me*, uncle! I don't know what these murdering Red Sleeves are going to get you, but I'm going to knock some spokes out of your wheel now!"

Dawson heaved a long sigh and sank back into his chair. There were hard lines at the corners of his mouth. "I'm afraid you're not going to do any of those things, Philip. You and your interfering government man have caused us enough trouble already. If you were anything but my own flesh and blood—"

"Family ties were not weighing heavily on your mind when you turned Moxelli loose on me this morning," said Philip.

"We had to get Seaver," said Dawson coldly. "He would have done too much talking."

"I'm going to do the talking now," said Philip grimly. He turned to go, and stopped abruptly. Standing in the doorway were two men—two very hard-looking men. One of them held an automatic.

"You see, Philip," said Dawson, "we can't let you go anywhere."

Philip Jaxon had never been one to hesitate in a tight spot. Dawson had scarcely stopped speaking when Philip swarmed on the man with the gun. A vicious kick knocked the gun ceiling-ward. A savage right uppercut sent the man's head smashing back against the door. And then it was all over. The second man brought a blackjack down on Philip's skull.

H.R. Dawson looked at the prone figure of his nephew. He smiled very faintly. "Too bad," he said. "We could use some of that fervor in our cause."

CHAPTER VIII

"SCRAM"

REMSEN LOOKED AT the man with the cold blue eyes who stood on the doorstep of the Dawson home. The butler's face did not alter a shade in expression as he said:

"Mr. Philip Jaxon has not been here today at all, sir."

Dominick Vane's eyes seemed to bore into the man in a long, searching look. "That's very strange," he said. "I had an appointment with him here this morning." He hesitated a moment. "I wonder if I might speak to Miss Angela Dawson?"

"Who shall I say is calling, sir?"

"Simply say it's a friend of Mr. Jaxon's and that I have an important message for her."

"Very good, sir."

Dominick Vane waited in the little reception hall. Presently Angela Dawson came down the stairs. As she saw Vane her face brightened. "This *is* a surprise," she said. "Why didn't you send up your name?"

"I didn't think you'd remember," said Dominick Vane.

"I'm glad you are all right after your terrible experience in Marshfield. And the dreadful story in the paper this morning about the pineys! You're going to tell me what it all means?"

Vane looked meaningly at Remsen who stood respectfully by. "I'm very anxious to talk to you alone," he said.

"But of course. We'll go into the library. Can I have Remsen bring you something? Or do you drink highballs in the morning? I'm a little vague about what you do to entertain gentlemen visitors at this hour of the day."

"You just talk to them," said Dominick Vane.

Angela led the way to the library, a cool, high-ceilinged room, and made a place for Vane beside her on an upholstered lounge. "I've really been terribly anxious about you and Philip," she said.

"It's about Philip I've come," said Dominick Vane grimly. "But first I want to ask you a few questions if I may. Miss Dawson, you are H.R. Dawson's ward, not his daughter—isn't that so?"

She nodded. "My father and mother were friends of Mr. Dawson's. They died when I was a baby and Mr. Dawson adopted me. He's not really my father. But he has been pretty swell to me, Mr. Vane. Why do you ask?"

"Because I'm going to say things to you that you won't believe," Vane said, "and I wanted to know exactly where I stood. But first more questions. How long has Remsen been with you?"

"Almost since I can remember," said Angela. "Twenty years or more."

"He'd carry out orders unquestioningly?"

"Of course."

Dominick Vane's lips tightened perceptibly. "And now for one last question. Have you seen Philip here this morning?"

Angela's eyes widened. "No. And I would have had he been here, Mr. Vane."

Dominick Vane lit a cigarette and dragged hungrily on it for a moment, his eyes averted from the girl's lovely face.

"I warned you I was going to tell you things you wouldn't believe," he said, "so here goes."

VANE TOLD her about the visit of Dawson and Moxelli to Marshfield. He told her about the murder of the stable boy and the animals. He told her about the machine-gunner in the death car who had mowed down Morse and Seaver.

"But, Mr. Vane, this is all too incredible!" Angela broke in.

"I'm going to tell you more incredible things than that," he said harshly. "Things that will hurt. Can you take it, Angela Dawson?" He met her eyes steadily.

"I can take it," she said quietly. "Something has happened to Philip."

Dominick wondered why he felt a sudden sharp spasm of jealousy at her obvious alarm. Angela Dawson meant nothing to him.

"I don't know if something has happened to Philip. That's why I'm here," he said. "And here's the part that's going to hurt. I'm firmly convinced that your guardian is the financial power behind these Red Sleeves who, if Seaver's story is correct, mean to throw this country into a reign of bloody terror within a very few days. His connection with Moxelli is too much of a coincidence to overlook. Philip came here this morning to try and find out the truth. I was to meet him later at the University Club to hear the results. He didn't show up, so I came here after him. Remsen told me he had never been here."

Angela Dawson's hand closed tightly over Vane's wrist. "Something must have happened to him on the way! Oh, Mr. Vane, I simply can't believe this about Mr. Dawson. You're wrong there. But these people—these other people—must have done something to Philip before he could get here."

Dominick Vane shook his head grimly. "He got here all right, Miss Dawson. I had him followed! My man saw Remsen let him into the house. He hasn't come out."

Angela Dawson stared at him with horror-struck eyes. "Then—then—"

"I wonder if you'd have Remsen in here for a minute. You ask him if Philip has been here."

"Of course." Vane watched her as she rose to ring the bell. Plenty of nerve there, he thought. A swell girl!

A moment later Remsen came into the room. "Yes, Miss Angela?"

"Remsen, has Mr. Philip been here this morning?"

There was the barest hesitation. Then Remsen said, "No, Miss Angela."

Angela Dawson's voice hardened. "Remsen, Mr. Vane *knows* that Mr. Philip came here this morning. He was followed. The man who followed him saw you let him in."

Remsen looked down at the polished toes of his shoes. "The man was mistaken, Miss Angela."

Dominick Vane had been standing slightly behind the butler as Angela questioned him. Now his hand shot out, clapped the butler on the shoulder, and spun him around. "Remsen," he said grimly, "if you're in this mess yourself I know you won't talk. But if you're not—if you're just following orders you don't understand—I want to tell you that Mr. Jaxon's life is in immediate danger."

Remsen's lips quivered. "I—I—"

"You've got to tell me what you know, man," said Dominick Vane. "Do you want to be responsible for Philip Jaxon's death?"

"But—I—I—"

"Remsen, you must tell us!" said Angela tensely.

Remsen's voice shook. "This may mean my position, Miss Angela. But if what you say is true...."

"It *is* true," said Vane sharply.

"Mr. Philip did come here this morning," said Remsen resignedly. "He went directly to Mr. Dawson's study. I didn't see him leave, but a little later Mr. Dawson came to me and gave me orders to tell anyone who might inquire that Mr. Philip hadn't been here. He said it was of the utmost importance, I hate to think what he'll say when he knows I've told you."

"Where is Mr. Dawson now?" Vane asked.

"He's still in the study, sir. He's in some kind of a business conference with Mr. Corbett and Mr. Frampton."

Corbett and Frampton! Two famous Wall Street names! Dominick Vane's lips were tightly set. "I must see him at once," he said.

"Oh, but you can't interrupt him now, sir. He—"

"Where is the study?"

"I'll show you," said Angela Dawson decidedly.

SHE LED the way across the hall, Remsen hovering in the background literally wringing his hands. Without bothering to knock, Vane wrenched open the door and stepped across the threshold.

H.R. Dawson looked up, an angry glitter in his gray eyes. John Corbett, dapper, dark steel-operator, and Paul Frampton, tall, rangy, leather-faced oilman, were seated on either side of the desk. At the sight of Angela directly behind Vane, Dawson checked what had started to be an angry exclamation. There was still an edge to his voice despite his politeness.

"Angela, dear, you know that when I'm in conference I—"

Dominick Vane cut in harshly: "Dawson, what have you done to Philip Jaxon?"

Very slowly Dawson shifted his gaze from Angela to the federal man, and there was a cold, suppressed fury in them. "I don't think I understand," he said.

"What have you done to Jaxon?" Vane repeated, enunciating very slowly and clearly.

"My dear fellow," Dawson drawled, "I haven't the faintest idea what you're talking about. Philip hasn't been here today."

"Oh, uncle," Angela cried, in a strangled voice, "what have you done? Remsen has already told us that Philip came here and saw you. Is it possible that what Mr. Vane has been telling me is true?"

"So Mr. Vane has been telling you things, eh?" Dawson said very quietly. He reached quickly across the desk and picked up the telephone. "I want the long distance operator for Washington, D.C.," he said. His eyes were fixed on Vane as he spoke. "I want to speak personally in Washington with Mr. Corcoran, Chief of the Division of Investigation of the Department of Justice. Corcoran... that's right. Yes, I'll hold the wire." He covered the mouthpiece with his hand. "I've had just about enough of your nonsense, Vane," he said grimly.

He turned back to the phone and a moment later the call was connected. "Corcoran? This is H.R. Dawson. That's right. Oh, I'm fine, but I'm very annoyed with one of your men. Chap named Vane. Yes. I told you only yesterday of his unwarranted inclusion of my nephew in a dangerous business out in Jersey. Well, he's gone that one better. He's standing here now accusing me of having *done* something to my nephew. Do you have many lunatics in your division? Eh? Now get this, Corcoran. Call off your dog! And get this too. Unless that fellow is dismissed from the service immediately I'll turn your department upside down… I see… Very good I'd be glad if you'd relay those orders to him now… over this phone." Dawson calmly handed the instrument across the desk to Vane, whose jaw muscles rippled under the tan of his cheeks Dawson was smiling—a triumphant smile.

"Hello, Corky?" Dominick Vane's voice was hard.

Corcoran's reply was one sharp word: "Scram!" he said.

"But, Corky, listen. I—"

"Get out of that house just as fast as you can leg it," said Corcoran, "and take the first plane you can get back to Washington." The receiver clicked at the other end.

Vane put down the telephone. He was angry, bitterly disappointed, and alarmed at the danger Philip was in. But orders were orders.

"Have you anything more to say, Mr. Vane?" Dawson drawled.

"Nothing," said Vane, between his teeth. He turned away. "Goodbye, Miss Dawson," he said to Angela.

"I'll see you to the door," said the girl.

"Angela!" Dawson's voice cracked sharply. "I want you to wait here!"

Without giving him a look the girl went out into the hall with Vane, shutting the study door a little more firmly than was necessary. Her hand slipped quickly into Vane's and she looked up at him with frightened eyes.

"You were right!" she whispered. "He's in it!"

"Up to his neck!" Vane said shortly. He felt his heart beating a little unsteadily as he looked down into the lovely upturned face of the girl. "I wish you were out of this house—away from him," he said with sudden passion. "I've got to go back to Washington. Orders. Apparently Dawson has all kinds of pull. I may sound mad to you… but if you'd come with me…."

"Philip's here somewhere," she said. "Somebody's got to do something for him. If you can't, I must."

He looked at her wonderingly. "Aren't you frightened?"

"To death," she said, with a tremulous little smile.

From his pocket Vane took a pencil and a torn scrap of paper from an envelope. He scribbled something on it. "If you need me," he said, "call this number in Washington, and I'll come to you. It looks as if I were going to get the sack anyhow. If I do I'm coming back for Philip on my own. Let me know what happens here."

Her hand tightened around his fingers for a moment. "I will, Dominick," she said.

Then Vane did something that lie tried for the next three hours to explain to himself. He bent down and kissed her.

"Goodbye, Angela," he said.

CHAPTER IX

MOBILIZATION

IN THE PRIVATE study of the President of the United States at the White House in Washington a conference was in session. In addition to the Chief Executive himself were the Secretary of State, the Secretary of War, the Secretary of the Navy, General Barrett, Chief of the Military Intelligence, Admiral Hewitt, Chief of the Naval Intelligence, and Michael Corcoran, Chief of the Investigation Division of the Department of Justice.

Corcoran, his stiff leg stuck out in front of him, had been holding the floor, his fingers caressing the game leg as he talked. "Those are the facts as I know them," he said in conclusion. "Some of them may sound fantastic to you, gentlemen, but they are the report of a man who has been one of the best operatives in the department. And you cannot get behind the known parts of the story—the wholesale slaughter of these pineys; the shell holes in the middle of the barrens."

The President was tapping a pencil nervously on the blotter in front of him. "What I cannot understand, Mr. Corcoran," he said, "is how an organization as large as you claim for the Red Sleeves could exist without some word of it having reached us before this Marshfield business. You may recall that last February the House appointed a Committee to investigate anti-American activities in the country—the McCormack Committee. They reported on many things. They even mentioned a militant group who called themselves the Silver

Shirts. But there was no mention of the Red Sleeves, who must have been in existence if they are as powerful as you suggest."

Corcoran shifted restlessly in his chair. "Mr. President, with unlimited wealth and influence behind them they could have kept things secret. General Barrett and Admiral Hewitt will back me up in one respect, I think. We know for certain that this group of Red Sleeves in Marshfield had rifles, artillery, poison gas, gas masks, and other equipment. The whole facilities of the Military and Naval Intelligence have been trying to discover the source of this equipment without any success whatever. Am I right?"

General Barrett nodded. "Complete blank up to now, sir," he told the President. "But we have unearthed hints and a few clues here and there that led us to think there have been other drill grounds for these men. In the hills back of San Diego our men report finding shell holes in the ground and many dead animals in the woods. Similar reports have come from Wisconsin in the North, Louisiana and Texas in the South, and from Vermont in New England. We cannot say whether these are the only centers of activity or whether there are hundreds more that we know nothing about."

"But where does the money come from?" the President asked. "They cannot have raised funds publicly."

Corcoran's lips tightened. "This agent of mine, Dominick Vane, has hit on one source, he believes, with absolute certainty. He tells me that H.R. Dawson is behind this thing."

The President threw back his head and laughed. "Dawson!... My dear Corcoran, I'm inclined to think this agent of yours is a trifle unbalanced. Dawson!... Good Lord, man, don't you know that revolution would strike first at capitalists of Dawson's stature?"

"Some kinds of revolution might, sir," said Corcoran earnestly. "But if Vane is right this business is directed at you and your government, Mr. President. It is not a communistic effort, sir.

It is an organized attempt to turn over the reins of power to another group—a group of dictators."

"Is there any basis of fact in your agent's suspicion?" the President asked.

"A man named Moxelli visited Marshfield with Dawson," said Corcoran. "This morning that same Moxelli was recognized as the machine-gunner in a murder car who shot down and killed one of my agents and a man named Seaver who gave us our first clue to the Red Sleeves. Vane and Philip Jaxon, Dawson's nephew, who has been working with Vane, escaped." Corcoran paused. "We have records on this man Moxelli. He was suspected of being connected with a huge drug ring at one time. He is known to be a drug addict himself. He has been close to half-a-dozen brutal crimes, though he's never been proven guilty. There could be no possible business connection between him and Dawson that was on the up-and-up. Yet Dawson claimed him as a business associate."

"There is probably some simple explanation of all this," said the President. "I simply cannot believe that a man of Dawson's standing could be involved."

"Is there any significance, sir," Corcoran said, "to the fact that Dawson telephoned me about two hours ago demanding that Vane be dismissed from the service?"

The President looked gravely at Corcoran. "Where is this man Vane?"

"I recalled him, sir. He should have arrived in Washington by now. I left word at my office for him to come here at once to make his report to you in person."

General Barrett leaned forward earnestly. "I do not believe, Mr. President, that this matter can be considered lightly. I am convinced with Corcoran that there is a dangerous storm brewing and that even now we may have learned of it too late to prevent its breaking."

"I concur in that belief," said Admiral Hewitt gravely.

At that moment one of the President's secretaries came into the room. "Mr. Dominick Vane, sir."

"Show him in at once," said the Chief Executive.

DOMINICK VANE came into the study. His cold blue eyes swept the faces of the men assembled. He knew them all by sight and Barrett and Hewitt personally. Vane's face was very pale and his left arm hung limply at his side. At sight of him Corcoran sprang up out of his chair.

"Nick, you're hurt!" he said.

"Nothing much," said Dominick Vane. "Someone took a pot shot at me as I left the Department of Justice building to come here. Winged me in the left arm."

There was dead silence in the room for a moment. Then the President said very quietly. "I should like to hear your story in detail, Mr. Vane."

Dominick Vane began to talk in short, clipped sentences. He told them everything he knew, everything he suspected, everything he feared. "And at this time," he concluded bitterly, "Dawson still has enough influence with the Department to have me withdrawn from the case, with Jaxon's life in danger— without a chance to explain my suspicions."

"At this moment, Nick," said Corcoran softly, "your life is much more valuable to us than Philip Jaxon's. It was vital that you should come here in person to present your facts to the President."

"Then I'm not fired?" asked Dominick Vane eagerly. "I can go back after Philip?"

"Oh, you're fired all right, Mr. Vane," said the President of the United States. So stunned was Vane by this announcement that he failed to notice the twinkle in the Chief Executive's eyes. He listened dully as the President dictated a press statement to his secretary to the effect that Dominick Vane had been dropped from the Government Service for official reasons.

"I guess," said Vane grimly, "that I won't be needed here any longer." He turned to go.

"Just a moment, Mr. Vane," said the President. He was smiling now, openly. "No man can hold two jobs, my friend, and do justice to them. That is why you have been dropped from the Department. I have a new commission for you.

"A new commission," said the President. "From now on, Mr. Vane, you will be in charge of a special division—a sort of flying squad of picked men—with special instructions to deal with this Red Sleeve menace. You will pick your own men—any number you wish from any branches of the service that you choose. You will act in any way you see fit, with full authority from me to follow whatever course of action seems best to you. You will be one of a committee of five, including myself, General Barrett, Admiral Hewitt, and Corcoran, empowered to deal with this business. You will make your reports to Corcoran or to me, as you think best or as is most convenient."

There was a glitter of excitement in Dominick's eyes. "Thank God, Mr. President, you recognize the danger with which we are confronted," he said fervently. "When does this commission take effect?"

"At once. You will consult with Barrett, Hewitt and Corcoran about the men you want under your immediate command. We count on you to crush this thing in the bud."

"I only hope we are not too late, sir!" Vane said.

ON UPPER Fifth Avenue in New York stood a great, square, stone house. It appeared innocent enough, this house. Riders on the bus-tops could see over a high stone wall into a little green patch of garden. Perhaps they wondered who, in these days of reduced fortunes, had money enough to keep up such an establishment. One thing they never dreamed was that here was the center of a sinister plot aimed to strike at the very life blood of the country. That here was the headquarters of the Red Sleeves. No one had heard of the Red Sleeves at that time, yet in a few hours that name was destined to strike terror into the hearts of people the length and breadth of a great nation.

In a high-ceilinged library of this house stood a man who

was studying his own reflection in a full length mirror set into a panel in the wall. No one could deny that his appearance was arresting. Tall, gaunt, perhaps fifty odd years of age, his face was deeply lined. His eyes were deep-set and burning, and a psychiatrist must have recognized in them the light of an unbalanced mind. His lower lip jutted out, giving to his face an arrogant tyrannical look. He was dressed in gray riding-pants with shiny, black boots. He wore a gray-flannel shirt with a black tie, and around each sleeve above the elbow was a brilliant crimson arm band. The left sleeve was empty, pinned to the side of the shirt.

America knew this man. They knew that arm had been shot away in France. They knew that the World War had made him one of the country's great military heroes. They knew that since then he had been the stormy petrel of the War Department. They knew that he had at one time attempted to form an organization of vigilantes to fight bootleggers in the dead days of prohibition. They knew him as a hero, as a martinet, as a rock-ribbed moralist, as a passionate patriot who had conceived it his duty to publicly denounce the new policies of the current administration in Washington. They knew that he had retired from the service to private life.

But there were things the public did not know about General Edward Ellison. They did not know that he was an exaggerated egomaniac, thirsting for power. They did not know that he spent hours before this full length mirror gazing at his own reflection. They did not know that General Ellison had become a powerful tool in the hands of an unscrupulous group of men bent on the destruction of a system of government that had stood firm for more than a hundred and fifty years.

General Ellison's contemplation of himself in the glass was interrupted by the entrance of a man who was also dressed in the gray uniform with the scarlet arm-bands.

"Mr. Dawson and the others to see you, General," he said.

Ellison turned from the glass. There was a perpetual deep scowl between those deep-set burning eyes.

"Show them in!"

He stood, legs spread apart, chest thrown out, the thumb of his hand slipped under the black belt he wore. As H.R. Dawson, Frampton and Corbett came into the room he held out his arm in a stiff gesture of salute.

"I was expecting you, gentlemen," he said. It was a crisp, resonant voice, used to commanding. "Your men have botched things!"

H.R. Dawson smiled that faint, almost mocking smile of his. "You mean *your* men, General," he said dryly. "Letting that government agent, Drewes, get away from Marshfield was the initial mistake."

"An unavoidable accident," said the general coldly. "But your stupidity, Mr. Dawson, in allowing yourself to be seen publicly with Moxelli has made it possible for the government to associate you with this venture before we are ready."

"I admit the mistake," said Dawson quietly. "But there is no use crying over spilled milk, General. We've had bad luck. Two attempts have been made on the life of this man Vane and both, unfortunately, have failed. We learn from Washington that he has had an audience with the President."

"How does that effect your plans, General?" dapper John Corbett asked.

ELLISON STRODE majestically up and down the thick Persian rug for a moment. "In five days we could have struck with complete assurance of success. In my judgment, gentlemen, to allow the government five days of preparation now might have serious consequences. It is true that certain vital preparations of ours are not completed, but without the element of surprise many important parts of our plan might fail."

Tall, angular, leather-faced Paul Frampton looked shrewdly at the general. "You think, then, that we should not delay?"

Ellison's eyes burned like red hot coals. "I think the signal to go should be given at once!" he said decisively.

The three rich men looked at each other in silent conference. It was Dawson who spoke: "We will need, General, about three hours to make certain financial arrangements. Since our connection with this affair may be known in Washington it seems important that we should liquidate certain assets before things begin."

"It will take at least that long before all the orders are passed along to our divisional commands," said Ellison. He glanced at a clock on the mantel. "It is now two P.M. I will give orders for Plan A to go into operation at precisely six P.M. Will that give you sufficient time, gentlemen?"

"It will," said Dawson.

Abruptly Ellison held out his arm in that stiff salute. His hand seemed to shake a little.

And a moment later from an upper room in that same Fifth Avenue house a telegraph operator tapped out the same message over and over:

Plan A at 17... Plan A at 17... Plan A at 17....

To San Francisco, to Denver, to Chicago, to Boston, to Dallas, to New Orleans, to Seattle, on and on to every part of the country that message went.

Plan A at 17... Plan A at 17....

IN A cottage in New England a wildly excited man came rushing into the room where his wife was patiently darning socks.

"It's come, Miriam!" he said. "The signal has come!"

Color left the woman's face.

"Tonight at six o'clock!" he said. "Thank God this long period of waiting is over."

The woman twisted her fingers tightly together in her lap. "I wish to heaven I could believe in this thing as you do, Ted. I wish I believed that this terrible violence could get us what we want! Can't we get the right men in power through elections? Must we have death and destruction?"

"We've tried to beat the political machines that way and we can't. Now we're going to use force!"

"But what's to become of me, Ted? We have so little now, and without you to earn something...."

"The family of every Red Sleeve will be cared for," the man cried. "They have promised us that. You'll be better off now than you've ever been!"

... Plan A at 17... Plan A at 17....

In a bar-room in New York a man rushed in, his cheeks flushed with excitement.

"Double rye and soda," he ordered. He glanced around, saw only one other man seated at a table some distance away, and spoke eagerly to the bartender. "It's come, George! *Plan A at Seventeen!* It's the end of waiting. We'll do for those bureaucrats in Washington who have been putting the screws on us for years. America for Americans! That's what we're going to have now!"

His voice had risen at the end so that the man at the table looked up. "Hello, Mr. Murcheson," he said. "What's all the excitement?"

Murcheson spun around from the bar and an evil grin spread over his face. He went quickly over to the table. "Well, well, well, if it isn't Mr. Ferretti, the grocer," he said, in a sneering voice. "Oh, there's excitement all right, Ferretti. Plenty of excitement. America for Americans, that's what it is. No place for foreigners like you!"

"I guess you must be drunk," said Ferretti calmly.

"Drunk! Ha! You damn foreigner calling me drunk, eh?" Out shot his fist and knocked the other man sprawling over backward in his chair. Before Ferretti could pick himself up, the man Murcheson had grabbed another chair and brought it smashing down over the prostrate man's head... once, twice, three times until it splintered in his hands. Ferretti lay still, his head bloody and battered.

"Gee, Murch, the cop'll get you for that," said the frightened bartender.

"Cops! That's a laugh, George! By tomorrow there won't be any cops, the graft-taking, crooked lice! We won't have to worry about cops any more, George!"

… Plan A at 17… Plan A at 17….

Moxelli lay stretched out on a sofa in a lavish west-side apartment, squinting along the barrel of a revolver he held loosely in his hand. He, too, was dressed in the gray uniform and red armbands of a Red Sleeve. The gray-flannel shirt accentuated the flabbiness of his stomach. His thick lips were twisted into that curious little one-sided smile, and from time to time his greedy little black eyes glanced in the direction of a girl who stood with her back to the table in the center of the room.

"Pretty soon we'll be big shots, my sweet," said Moxelli in that soft, purring voice of his.

"That's fine," said the girl in a flat voice.

"I'm telling you," said Moxelli softly, "because you're supposed to know that a big-shot's girl mustn't have a word of scandal breathed about her. You understand, my sweet?"

"Of course, Mox—of course I understand." There was stark fear in the girl's voice—in her eyes.

Moxelli swung his feet off the lounge and stood up. He slipped the revolver into a holster at his side and walked with that slow, catlike tread over to the girl. His great hands hung loosely at his sides.

"You've got to try to forget what you are," said Moxelli softly. "You've got to remember what will happen to you if I hear of you pulling anything. Something like this!" One of his hands flashed out and struck the girl a stinging blow across the mouth. A little trickle of blood ran down her chin. Moxelli laughed. "You won't forget, will you, my sweet?"

"No, Mox." It was a whisper.

"I've got to be going," he said. "Read the morning papers if you want to know how I'm going, my pet."

IN THE offices of the M.I.D. in Washington Dominick Vane was closeted with General Barrett. Vane looked drawn and tired but his eyes had a bright, feverish light in them. During that afternoon he had selected the force of men to work under him in his new command. About twelve of them were from his own Department, about twenty from the combined forces of the Military and Naval Intelligence; four others were private investigators whom Vane knew by reputation.

"We should be ready to function within twenty-four hours," said Dominick Vane. It was then five o'clock in the afternoon. "You have a clear picture, General Barrett, of the military situation in the whole country. I'd like to know about that. I'd like to know just what we can count on from the army if it comes to a showdown."

There was a great map spread out on Barrett's desk. The chief of the M.I.D. puffed methodically on his pipe as he talked. "We're operating under The Four Army plan which was recently put into effect," he said. "Each of these Armies has an assigned area of the States. The First Army covers roughly New England and the Middle Atlantic States—as you see here. Headquarters at Governors Island in New York. The Second Army covers the Middle West with headquarters at Chicago. The Third Army covers the Texas border and the Southwest, with headquarters at Fort Sam Houston in San Antonio. The Fourth Army covers the Pacific with headquarters at San Francisco."

"I see," said Vane. "And how many men can be counted on for immediate action?"

Barrett looked a little grim as he held a match to his pipe. "The regular army," he said, "numbers only about 120,000 men. A year or so ago when there was a scare about a communist revolution it was said that it would take 165,000 regular army men to handle the situation along with the National Guard, which lumbers about 185,000. Then there is the organized Reserve.

There are about 90,000 officers in this division but practically no men. Of course many civilians have had military training and would be drafted in time of war."

"I see." Vane looked thoughtful.

Barrett gave him a quick look. "Has it occurred to you, Mr. Vane, that we have no way of knowing how many of this number, outside the regular army, we can count on. The Red Sleeves have been drilling. How many Reserve Officers and National Guardsmen have they in their outfit? If we were attacked by an alien army we could count on them all! But what of a cancerous rebellion like this? From what you tell me they have some pretty fine phrases about America for Americans, and down with an outmoded political machine and all that sort of thing. We've been through a pretty thin time in this country, Mr. Vane. I should hate to make an estimate of how many of these non-regulars would stand by the Government. They'll look on it as a family row. Both sides will be shouting their heads off about patriotism."

VANE NODDED. "Of course you're right," he said. He brought his closed fist impatiently down on the desk. "If the people could only be made to see that any scheme financed by Dawson and his crowd can have nothing but personal gain for its purpose."

"We have a propaganda department to handle that sort of thing," said Barrett. "But we'll have to work fast."

It was then twenty minutes past five.

"Can you make any sort of guess as to where the trouble might start?"

Barrett fussed with his pipe for a moment. "If they have a decently organized plan, and we think they have, it will start everywhere at once. It will have to, to have any chance of success. Of course the most dangerous places from our point of view are big cities. If they are equipped and provisioned they can subjugate the rest of the population by cutting off food supplies. They could draw thousands of recruits to their cause if it meant the difference between being fed and not being fed."

"Naturally. It would be up to the military to see that the food supplies were not interfered with."

"It would," said Barrett grimly. "And there are other crucial points that a revolutionary body would attempt to seize or destroy, such as the Niagara Falls power-plant; the Springfield arsenal; the General Electric plant at Schenectady; the Du Pont works; the Bethlehem Steel plants. If they could get control of these key situations it would give them tremendous power. If they could destroy them, we'd be—"

"General, we've got a job on our hands! When you see it in all its details it puts fear into you!" Vane said.

Barrett nodded. "If the Red Sleeves are as strong as you think they are, Mr. Vane, we're in for no tea party!"

Twenty minutes to six.

"Washington itself," said the general, "may be a danger spot. The quickest thing they could do for their cause would be crack down on the government officials here. Congress is in session and they might try to wipe out as many of them as possible. Every moment from now on the President is in the most terrible danger of assassination. He laughed it off when I told him so this afternoon. But it's true. In a mess like this no one is to be thoroughly trusted until the Red Sleeves have come out into the open."

Dominick Vane stood up. "We'll do a little cracking-down of our own, General. In the morning I'm heading for New York with a squad of my men to turn the heat on Dawson and his crowd, including Moxelli, Brace and all his killers. Meanwhile all military headquarters have been warned of the danger?"

"They have," said Barrett. "In a day or two they should be fully prepared."

It was then ten minutes to six.

CHAPTER X

REVOLUTION!

AT SIX O'CLOCK the United States turned into a madhouse! And the man who pulled the strings was the maddest of all. But he possessed a cunning and skill that could only spring from a warped brain—from an ego as inflated as was that of General Edward Ellison.

At six o'clock began a reign of terror such as the country had never dreamed could happen. From coast to coast, in every city of any size, in every critical sector of the whole great nation, the Red Sleeves showed their colors. Newspaper offices were seized and copy prepared long in advance was rushed onto the presses in some cases by willing workmen, in other cases by men who worked at gunpoint.

Radio stations were suddenly raided by armed men, and Red Sleeve propaganda was broadcast from coast to coast. Ellison had organized beforehand a secret General Staff. Moxelli was chief of the "shock troops," prepared to drive or fly to any danger point to lend their weight in dangerous sectors. An intelligence staff under the guidance of Lefty Brace had gathered a mass of data on public officials, judges, police chiefs, railway, telegraph, aviation, electricity, gas, water works, coast guard, army and navy. Every large city had been carefully charted with special attention to industrial centers, police stations, military posts, railroad stations, banks, post and telegraph offices, and all main roads leading into towns. Thus with every scrap of information at its fingertips the Red Sleeves were able to strike a crushing blow in a minimum of time.

Washington, as Barret had predicted only a few moments before, was in chaos. Dominick Vane had been walking on foot from the M.I.D. offices to his apartment when things broke. Dazed, scarcely believing what he saw, he was crowded into a doorway by a mob of panic-stricken citizens fleeing for their lives. Up Pennsylvania Avenue swept a solid phalanx of armored-cars, spouting death and destruction from behind their armor plate. Behind them came a smartly drilled regiment of Red Sleeves heading grimly for the White House. A shrieking, singing rabble followed, shouting hysterical curses on the head of the government. Stones were hurled through windows—bullets spattered against the facades of government buildings.

Dominick Vane had to fight his way through the crowd in the direction of his apartment. He thought if he could get to the telephone there and send orders quickly to his men at headquarters he would save time. It was easy to see the purpose behind this merciless attack on the innocent people on the streets. Strike terror enough into their hearts in one awful night and there would be thousands upon thousands who would turn to the Red Sleeve cause rather than run the risk of slaughter at their hands.

It is at such times that men rise to heroic heights undreamed of before. Later on there were fabulous tales of things that had happened during the first hectic hours of the revolution. They told of the gallant fight made by the special White House police who fought like fiends, hiding behind pillars and posts, shooting from windows, actually emerging for hand-to-hand combat with the superior forces of the Red Sleeves who swarmed across the White House grounds. They told of the President himself calmly walking through the building urging everyone else to run for safety and let him take what was coming to him. They told of the miraculous speed with which the Third Cavalry and the Sixteenth Artillery rushed men to the aid of the beleaguered chief executive. People afterwards recalled how General MacMaster himself, Chief of Staff of the Army, led a troop of cavalry straight into the ranks of the Red Sleeves, fighting and slashing with their heavy-hilted sabres. Fifteen minutes after the fighting started the Sixteenth Artillery had managed to turn a half dozen .75s on the revolutionists, sweeping their ranks with bursts of shrapnel.

Meanwhile Dominick Vane had reached his apartment and rushed frantically for the telephone. The wire was dead. He could not know that ten minutes before the Washington telephone exchange had been destroyed by a time bomb evidently placed there days before and set ahead in the emergency by some agent of the Red Sleeves in the building. Hundreds of telephone girls had been ruthlessly slaughtered. He could not know that telegraph operators lay dead at their instruments while Red Sleeves replaced them and sent news of the progress of affairs in Washington to their mates in other cities. All lines of communication into the nation's capital were either destroyed or in the hands of the Red Sleeves.

But as Vane presently discovered, those lines of communication had not been disrupted a half an hour before. His Japanese servant, shaking with terror, had a message for him.

"A lady call you—half hour since," he chattered.

"The hell with ladies:" Vane said. "I've got to get to Corcoran's office."

"She say of excessive importance," said the Tapanese. "Name of Dawson."

"*What?*"

"She say danger to her is excessive. Can you if please come at once."

"Oh!…" Vane plunged out through the door of his apartment on the run.

IN HIS office at the Department of Justice Building, Corcoran paced the floor like a caged lion. From time to time men rushed in with reports. News from the White House had been grim for awhile but apparently that danger was over for the moment. The first attack of the Red Sleeves had been repulsed and the President was momentarily safe. No one knew what was happening in the rest of the country. Fliers had been dispatched from Washington to cities northward to carry and fetch what information was available. One man ducked back with news that the Red Sleeves had planes in the air and were attacking the commercial planes that attempted flight.

And then Dominick Vane, looking like a ghost, burst into the office.

"At last you're here!" Corcoran cried. "A dozen of your new division are waiting for orders."

"They can wait!" Vane cried hoarsely. "I came here to tell you I'm on my way, Corky. I'm chucking the whole thing, if necessary. I've got to get to New York. Angela phoned just before hell started popping. She needs me."

"Don't talk rot," Corcoran rapped. "You're needed here desperately. They've got the jump on us, these Red-Sleeved devils. We need every man with brains and courage here. You and your flying squad may be the difference between life and death to the President."

"I don't give a damn!" Vane said wildly. "Angela's in a jam!

Oh, I know I sound crazy. I only met the girl a few days ago but I know I don't give a hoot for anything else. I'm going, Corky."

Corcoran grabbed him roughly by the arm. "You're going to do no such thing," he said grimly. "Are you going to desert your country because some miserable skirt lets out a yip for help?"

"Don't talk to me that way, Corky," Vane said, a dangerous light in his eyes. "I'm going."

"The devil you are," said Corcoran. He took one stiff legged step forward and jammed his fist squarely into Vane's mouth. It was so unexpected that Vane's legs buckled under him and he fell. Instantly Corcoran was kneeling beside him.

"Gosh, I'm sorry, Nick. But you can't go! Don't you understand?"

Vane shook his head and raised himself up on his elbow. He looked steadily at Corcoran for a minute. "You're right, of course, Corky," he said, quietly. And then a passionate anger welled up into his throat. "But if anything has happened to her I'll tear Dawson limb from limb!"

"Your men are waiting for orders," said Corcoran grimly.

ONLY A few minutes later Dominick Vane, white, haggard, but with that diamond-hard light burning in his cold blue eyes faced the bulk of the men who were to operate under him as a special flying squadron—the pick of the special services of the country. They were a splendid group; highly trained with the courage and strength of tempered steel, and yet as Vane's eyes surveyed them he felt a sense of almost pitiful inadequacy. Only an hour or two ago it had seemed to him that they would be capable of dealing with the situation—that they would be able to sink their fingers into the throat of the Red Sleeve organization before it could get under way.

But there had been this unbelievable and sudden kaleidoscopic change in the situation. Even now they could hear the sound of gun fire outside. The Red Sleeves had swept down on Washington with the suddenness of a hawk wheeling down out of the sky on its victim.

"Gentlemen," said Dominick Vane, his voice hoarse with fatigue and anxiety, "when we formed this squad a few hours ago it was for the purpose of undermining this rebellion before it started. We are too late for that. The streets of Washington are running with blood at this moment; every other great center in the country has been dealt the same sudden, savage blow. We are not in possession of all the facts and may not be for weeks because of the completeness with which the Red Sleeves have taken over means of communication.

"Gentlemen, were it not for one single factor I would say that it was too late for this body to be of any use; I would say that we should all grab rifles and fall into the loyal ranks of soldiers who will fight hand to hand with these devils. That factor, gentlemen, is my firm belief that the great body of this revolutionist group has been grossly deceived by their higher ups!"

"Deceived?" It was Johnny Harbold, a young federal agent Vane knew personally and had picked for this job because of his red-headed impetuosity and daring.

"Precisely," said Dominick Vane. "These men believe they are fighting for a cause. They are not! They are fighting for a group of unscrupulous financiers who are using a man as their tool. I'm talking about Ellison. General Ellison plans to be dictator of the country—an American Hitler. But behind him are H.R. Dawson, John Corbett, Paul Frampton, and possibly other financial giants who are really in control. The honest revolutionists are fighting for something resembling a communist state—fighting to overthrow the system which they believe lies at the bottom of their ills. But actually, unknown to them, they are simply fighting to give a few unscrupulous capitalists absolute power. The leaders close in command to General Ellison, are criminals who actually are taking their orders from Dawson and Company—Moxelli. Brace, and I don't know how many more of their stamp. Ellison is so blind—so consumed with his own dream of power—that he doesn't realize that he is no more than a figurehead!"

"What a set-up!" said Johnny Harbold. "Any notion as to how large a force the Red Sleeves are?"

"None, as yet," said Dominick Vane. "Anything from a hundred and fifty thousand up to half a million would be a good guess, I should think. But they're organized—thoroughly organized and armed. They've been preparing for this for a long time, and they've caught us unprepared!"

"And *how!*"

"I should think a large percentage of their force would be paid gunmen, criminals, and riffraff of one sort or another. The rest of them are honest but misguided citizens—but they're up to their ears in a sort of frenzied, patriotic fervor! Talk isn't going to get anywhere with them. Fighting and resistance of a physical nature is only going to stir them to greater frenzy! But there is a way, gentlemen, that this thing can be dealt a death blow! Get the truth about their leaders before the rank and file of the Red Sleeves. It won't be sufficient to make claims about them. We've got to have proof—positive, irrefutable proof! That's our job, gentlemen."

"Where do we begin?" asked Johnny Harbold.

"We've got to find out what Dawson and Company have been promising for their adherents' support. We've got to find them, themselves. They're hiding out—keeping in the background. We've got to strike at Moxelli, Lefty Brace and the other criminals in the organization. We've got to find out where the weak links are in their plan so that our forces can strike at those spots. We've got to locate the Red Sleeve headquarters. We've got to open up as many avenues of propaganda for our own uses as possible." He paused and lit a cigarette. "I've got a set of orders here. New York, I believe, is the center of trouble at the moment. I'm going there with Johnny Harbold. Dugan and Ives. Cullinan, you, Healy and Rethberg will light out for Chicago…" And he went on with his list of assignments.

"About reports…" said Cullinan, when the orders were complete.

IT WAS then that Corcoran, who had remained quietly in the background, limped forward. His rugged Irish face was deeply lined, grave.

"You birds have got to know just what you're in for," he said quietly. "The government is back of you, but frankly, that doesn't mean much. This is a state of war, and your position is not materially different from that of spies in war time. Normal means of communication are not to be trusted. You men will be our greatest weapon against the Red Sleeves."

Somebody laughed. "The army and navy aren't going to be exactly chummy with them."

The gravity of Corcoran's manner increased. "I wonder if you men realize the situation as it concerns the army and navy," he said slowly. "In reality the Red Sleeves are a minority—but an armed and organized minority that numbers only fighting men in its ranks. There will be millions and millions of loyal citizens everywhere, trapped by this armed and organized minority. Take New York, for example, packed with people who are loyal to the government, yet in the hands of the revolutionists. What can the army and navy do, gentlemen? They cannot bombard New York from sea or air, or with artillery, without killing hundreds of thousands of their own supporters. They are handcuffed, gentlemen. And because the Red Sleeves have struck all over the country at one and the same time they cannot concentrate a large force on any one place. They are called on to defend critical points—to give aid to loyal citizens—to them; but they cannot go in for the kind of warfare they would use against a foreign foe. In time, gentlemen, the army and navy might prevail, but in the meantime how many million lives will be lost in his bloody revolution?

"No, gentlemen, Dominick is right. You can strike at the heart of this thing by exposing the rotten and corrupt quality of its leadership. Show the misguided revolutionists what their cause *really* is and you will split the Red Sleeves in two. But this will be a tremendous task!" He took a handkerchief from his pocket and wiped beads of sweat from his forehead.

"As to reports… Dominick is sending you out in teams—much as we sent out spy teams in the war. When it comes time to report, then one of your team must bring that report personally to Washington. Trust no one! Telephones, telegraph and radio are dangerous. Report here in Washington to me, General Barrett, Admiral Hewitt, or the President himself!"

Corcoran looked out grimly over the group that faced him and Vane. "I'm not much on pep talks, boys," he said in a suddenly warmer key. "I don't like high-sounding or sentimental phrases. But I'm telling you this, honestly and without pretense. The future of this country—the future of the whole world—may depend on what you accomplish in the next few days. Get to it! And give 'em everything you've got!"

He turned to Dominick Vane and held out his hand. "Good luck, Nick. We're counting on you up to the hilt."

"I won't fail you, Corky," said Dominick Vane.

CHAPTER XI

"CAN'T HAPPEN HERE?..."

TWO ARMY PLANES waited to take Dominick Vane, Johnny Harbold, Dugan and Ives to New York. Under cover of darkness things had quieted somewhat in Washington. There were street fights here and there, but the actual hostilities between the Red Sleeves and the forces of law seemed stalemated. Troops and special police had protected and now guarded the White House and other government buildings. On the other hand, Red Sleeves were in possession of newspaper and telegraph offices, the demolished telephone exchange and many police precinct stations. It was rumored that raiding squads of the gray-shirted revolutionists were still moving from point to point, striking with suddenness and success.

Vane and his "team" were escorted to the airport under a heavily-armed guard of G-men. The airport had been held despite repeated attacks by the Red Sleeves and it was still possible for government officials to leave the city in army or navy planes, although all commercial passenger service had been discontinued.

"Any news from New York?" Vane asked the airport manager.

"Newark airport apparently in the hands of the Red Sleeves, sir," said the manager grimly. "No reports from Floyd Bennett Field either." He laughed nervously. "I don't know just where we'll be able to set you down safely, sir... in the dark."

At that point the pilot strolled up—a Captain Keeler. He shook hands with Vane. "We've got a bomber here that'll carry

82

all four of you, Mr. Vane. Regular airports seem to be out, but I have a suggestion. I used to go to a private school up near Yonkers. There's an enormous open field just beyond the end of the subway line at Van Cortlandt Park. We could land there easily enough and I think I can spot it all right."

"Perfect," said Vane. "That lands us right in the city. I'd been wondering about getting across from Jersey or Long Island. These devils will have grabbed bridges, tubes, and ferries first shot out of the box. Let's get going, Captain Keeler."

Up into the night the great bomber soared with the four special agents, and once more, on a journey, Dominick Vane slept. Weariness from the intense excitement of the last few days was like a drug to his jaded nerves. Below, the lights of Washington faded away, punctuated here and there by the red flares from burning buildings. Keeler flew his plane high and without lights. Earlier rumors of fighting planes manned by Red Sleeves were not to be ignored.

Not until they were about fifteen minutes from New York did the pilot reach out and touch Dominick Vane who was in the seat beside him. He could not be heard over the roar of the motors but his pointing finger was enough. The light of two planes flying below and off to the right were visible. Vane gave the pilot a questioning glance, and Keeler indicated a pair of earphones which the agent adjusted over his head.

"Scout planes," said Keeler. "They could fly circles around us. But they don't seem to see us. We're about a thousand feet over them and not showing any lights. Unless someone spotted us on the way up we may slip by—or we may slip by anyhow."

"And if they spot us?" Vane asked.

"Then it's going to be a warm evening," said Keeler, tight-lipped.

The scout planes apparently had not spotted the bomber as they flew in great circles below, and with every passing moment they were nearer their objective. New York—or rather the great glow of its lights—was plainly visible. And it seemed only a moment later to Vane that he got a glimpse of the fairylike span of the George Washington Bridge. Then Keeler's voice grated into his ear-phones.

"Got us!"

THE TWO scout planes, on their tail now were shooting up like rockets, it seemed. Keeler peered ahead of him into the darkness, throttle wide open. One of the Red Sleeve planes was already above them and in a minute Vane guessed that it would dive. An army bomber was fair game to those Red Sleeve pilots. They hovered overhead for a moment, poised like birds of prey waiting to dive. But it was Keeler who dove first. The nose of the bomber went down. With its motors roaring, and the wind whistling through its wires, the big plane went hurtling toward the earth. It was so breathtaking, so terrific, that for a moment Dominick Vane could not look back at the enemy. He could only cling to his seat and gasp. But when he did look back the two Red Sleeve planes were dangerously close, tearing after them, with little tongues of red flame spurting from their cockpits. Machine-gun fire!

Down, down, Keeler drove his plane, teeth set together like a vise, sweat running off his white face… and the city was racing up to meet them.

"Man!" Vane's voice was hoarse.

"I *think* I'm going to make it," said Keeler dryly. "That dark space below us must be the park! It's *got* to be the park!"

When it seemed that the ground must come up and smash them, Keeler managed to level off his plane. It was probably one of the wildest landings ever made. In frank anticipation of death Dominick Vane closed his eyes. The wheels touched earth and they seemed to bound back fifty feet into the air like some frightened antelope. Then they touched again and went bounding and bucking along the turf.

"The minute we step, make tracks," Keeler snapped. "Those birds will fly low over us and open up the works." The bomber came to a jolting stop and Vane was already clambering out of the machine with his three men close behind. And they ran blindly across that dark space of turf, not toward the lights of the city but toward a clump of distant woods. The two Red Sleeve planes were sweeping across the field now, flying not a hundred feet off the ground. Keeler was taxiing along, trying for a take-off. The big bomber was just rising when a hail of lead poured into it. It fluttered for a moment and then nosed into the ground. There were sudden flames....

Dominick Vane stopped his headlong flight. "We've got to go back," he panted. "Try to get Keeler out—"

Johnny Harbold's fingers bit into his arm. "Don't be a fool, Dominick! He wouldn't have crashed if they hadn't already got him."

They lay in the woods, watching the bomber blaze like a tinder box. They could see people running excitedly toward it. There was nothing they could do. Grimly they realized that no one life was worth anything in the struggle they faced. At last Vane spoke in a shaken voice.

"We'll have to split up here," he said. "You have orders. Tonight you'll comb the city—get every scrap of information you can. We'll meet at ten in the morning and compare notes. Set your watches by mine. It's exactly seventeen minutes past midnight."

"And the meeting place?" asked Johnny Harbold.

Dominick Vane laughed, a ragged, mirthless laugh. "Who knows what place will be safe?" he said. "We'd better set two or three alternative spots. Hotels, railroad stations, subways are out."

"Perhaps these bleedin' Red Sleeves won't be so hot for culture," said Johnny Harbold. "How about the public library?"

"Good," said Vane. "And if that is out we'll take some street corners at random. Fiftieth Street, beginning at Lexington and progressing across to Tenth Avenue. We'd surely be able to get together unmolested on one of those corners."

DOMINICK VANE had his own objective when he and his

men separated there in the woods at Van Cortlandt Park, an objective that nothing on earth could have kept him from heading for—the town house of H.R. Dawson where he had last seen Angela. Where she had been, no doubt, when she had sent him that call for help.

The trip down from Van Cortlandt was a nightmare which Dominick never remembered very clearly. There were no taxis— all had been commandeered by the Red Sleeves. He remembered trying the subway station. Men in gray uniforms were at the turnstiles, questioning everyone who went in, and Vane had slipped back up to the street. There were no questions he cared to answer. It would take him hours to walk downtown. At last he had quite calmly stolen a car, parked in front of an apartment house near Baker Field. All had gone well until, at a traffic light which turned red, a squad of Red Sleeves approached the car. They were armed and they looked plenty tough. Vane hesitated only a fraction of a second before stepping on the gas and shooting off down Broadway, a hail of lead following him. And there were motorcycles behind him! He swerved off into a side street, brought the car to a screeching stop, and sprang out. Dodging and ducking pursuers… in and out of alleyways… it seemed to him that it was hours!

In the end he had shaken them. He had trudged on, exhausted, but in his heart was a murderous fury against these devils that gave him strength. Always in the shadow of the buildings, always with a hand tight over the butt of his gun, he traveled on. And then at last he came to Dawson's house. It was dark. He had half expected to see Red Sleeve guards surrounding the house, but there were none. Yet to ring the front doorbell and stand there waiting for someone to answer would be foolhardy.

He slid down the service alley to the back door, hesitated a second and then tried the door. It was open! Vane flashed the tiny fountain-pen torch he carried. The kitchen was clean and bare. An alarm clock on the shelf had stopped at six o'clock. Vane felt a sudden sickening sensation at the pit of the stomach. Somehow he had known it would be like this. Yet he had hoped and prayed that there would be someone here—perhaps Remsen, the butler—who could tell him something.

Ten minutes later he had been from top to bottom of the great house. It was empty. There was a neatness about everything, a mocking sort of neatness which told of a carefully-planned departure.

"Angela! Where are you?" It was the hoarse, despairing whisper of a man who expects no answer.

One of two things almost always happen to a man in a moment of terrific stress such as Vane faced in that empty house. Either he goes completely to pieces or he gets a thorough grip on his nerves and his reason and begins to function at top efficiency.

Dominick, for just a minute or two, was acutely aware of the screaming protests of a body that had been driven beyond the limits of physical endurance—of nerves drawn so taut that one more call for effort would shatter them. In less than three days he had been through that awful visit to the Murder Farm in the Piney swamps—had been in the shadow of death when the Red-Sleeve poison gas had nearly done for him and Philip Jaxon; a few hours later he had seen the village of dead Pineys, and then the slaughter in Jaxon's stable; again he had barely escaped when Moxelli cut loose his murderous machine-gun fire on them as they left Seaver's apartment; he had been shot at in Washington and wounded, as his aching arm constantly reminded him; he had been a witness to the Red-Sleeve butchery in the streets of the capital; and he had escaped by the skin of his teeth from Keeler's plane and from the Red Sleeves who had chased him in the streets.

But there was Angela! It was anxiety for her, fear for her safety, her very life, that had brought him here through hazards that only a man of the sternest fiber could have met. Now this house, barren of any clue, mocked him with its placid silence.

FOR JUST a minute Dominick felt that he had no energy left with which to fight. Angela was gone, and Angela had become the hub of his universe. And then suddenly he saw clearly the issues he had to face. The cold, hard, shock-proof logic that had always been his greatest asset as a man-hunter, returned to him. He had kept going for *personal* reasons all his life. He had become a government agent for a personal reason—because his fiancée had been murdered; he had set out to catch the Red Sleeves in order to revenge Ted Drewes; he had come through hell to this house to find Angela. All these were trifling reasons, he realized. They were nothing in the face of the real issue, as he saw it now.

A country—his country—was in chaos. His country was facing horror and upheaval and death at the hands of unprincipled men who were camouflaging selfish motives with high-sounding, idealistic phrases. Part of his people were being hoodwinked, and the other part were to be clubbed into submission. And he, Dominick Vane, had been entrusted with the job of smashing this vicious force before it was too late! What did Angela's life matter—or Philip Jaxon's—or his own? *Nothing!* He had no right to think of himself, of his own heart, or of his life! His personal hatred for Dawson, or for Moxelli, or Brace, or for any of the others was a trifling matter compared with the necessity for beating their game. His cause was the American People! To swerve for one instant toward any personal motive was to be a traitor.

Subconsciously he raised his hand to his jaw, to the spot, still tender, where Corcoran had struck him. Good old Corky! He had seen then what Dominick Vane saw now. There had been no doubt in Corky's mind about the course an American must follow.

The sense of fatigue and over-taxed nerves left Dominick suddenly. His moment of weakness and despair passed. In that empty house a man was rehabilitated. He was ready to go on once more—alert, emotionless, unwavering. His mind was shut tight against the clangers of his own personal loves and hates. He was the servant of an ideal and he would never lose sight of it again.

His thoughts spurring him to action, he went over the house

once more. And this time every sense of the man-hunter was on the alert. Things that he had missed in his first mad dash from room to room searching for Angela began to tell him a story. Dawson's study, where only a few hours before he had faced the financier and his friends, had been carefully cleared of anything incriminating. Desk drawers were empty and a blackened pile of paper ashes on the hearth gave their own account of evidence destroyed.

Upstairs there was proof that Dawson had planned his departure. He had left clothes behind, but they were all neatly packed away in moth-proof bags. The shades had been carefully drawn…. But there was not a scrap of paper—not a single letter had the financier left for prying eyes.

DOWN THE hall, however, Dominick found another room which held evidence of a grimmer story: A rumpled bed… a pillow with dark bloodstains on it… an ash tray on a bedside-table brimming with cigarette butts. In another ash tray across the room were the dead ends of several cigars. If he read the signs aright, Dominick guessed that this was where Philip Jaxon had been held prisoner. Philip, injured about the head, had tossed on this bed, smoking an endless chain of cigarettes. Across the room had sat a cigar-smoking guard, barring the one avenue of escape.

And then he found Angela's room. By an effort of will he stifled the threat of his heart to beat a little faster as the faint scent of her perfume reached him. He was looking for a story here—and he found it. Angela had left hurriedly. There were signs of a few odds and ends having been thrown in a bag and the rest of her things left as they might always have been. Dominick stood in the center of that empty room for a moment, drawing the smoke from his cigarette deep into his lungs. Angela had known what was coming. She had phoned him in Washington. She might have guessed that at some time he would find himself in this room. Might she not have left some clue behind for him?

His eyes searched the room and rested finally on the little telephone table beside the girl's bed. Something drew him over to it. A cigarette box, half full, an ash tray, a copy of Sinclair Lewis' novel, *It Can't Happen Here*, a telephone pad bare of writing, a silver cigarette lighter—that was all.

He picked up the pad and examined the top sheet. Sometimes writing on the last page bears through to the next. But there was nothing decipherable. He lit a fresh cigarette from the stub of the one he had been smoking and stayed there, reluctant for some reason, to move. He thought it was rather ironic that Angela should have been reading Lewis' novel about America under a dictator on the very eve of that imaginary situation becoming an accomplished fact.

Suddenly he picked up the book and opened it to the fly leaf. In that instant his heart jammed hard against his ribs. There, written in pencil, was his own number in Washington. And beneath it was an address: *21909 West End Avenue, Apartment 9B.*

It could be pure chance. The address might have been written there before and have nothing to do with him. Yet, for no logical reason he could put forward, Dominick felt certain that this address had something to do with this situation. Perhaps Angela had phoned him in Washington to tell him something about it.

At any rate he couldn't overlook it. He must go to West End Avenue.

CHAPTER XII

LAND OF THE FREE....

IN THE COMFORTABLE library of a country house twenty miles outside the city limits H.R. Dawson sat in a wing chair that was drawn up before the fire that burned in a large open fireplace. John Corbett, the dapper steel-operator and Paul Frampton, gangling, leather-faced oilman, sat across the hearth from him.

At the back of the room were two other men in Red Sleeve uniforms. One of them sat at a radio receiving set, earphones over his head. Messages were coming in rapidly and as the operator wrote them down on slips of paper the second man brought them across the room to Dawson.

"Here's the straight dope from Washington," said H.R. Dawson, stroking his little gray mustache:

" '*Telephone, telegraph, and transportation systems destroyed. Government forces hold airport. Troops repelled our attack on White House. President still lives. Marshalling forces for second attack. Believed Dominick Vane and several of newly-formed flying squad set out for New York in army bomber.*' "

"Vane!" said Frampton sharply. "That man's a pest! He can't do us any harm, but he's a damned nuisance."

"Don't underestimate an enemy, Paul," said Dawson grimly. "This man Vane may cause us a lot of annoyance unless he's bottled up. He knows entirely too much."

"What he knows he's already passed on," said Corbett. "And so what? What harm can it do us? The first thing the govern-

91

ment would be expected to do would be to discredit the Red Sleeve movement. Nobody's going to believe it if they *do* drag our names into it."

"Perhaps you're right," said Dawson. "But I'd feel better if he was out of the way. There's something very purposeful about Mr. Dominick Vane. And the fellow seems to live a charmed life… Hello—here are some more reports."

As he read a slow smile of satisfaction widened the banker's mouth. "Listen to this, gentlemen:

"Du Pont works in our hands. Ammunition shipments to central points already begun by trucks under heavy guard!" And this: *Chicago: Thousands flocking to our cause here. Police badly routed in street fighting. Engagement with troops in Evanston resulted in partial victory for us. Airports in our hands. Propaganda spreading like wildfire finds citizens in receptive mood."*

Dawson shuffled the reports in his hands. "The same thing from all over the country, gentlemen. Ellison's fears seem to have been misplaced. Even though we were forced to strike sooner than we expected we have met with success all along the line. Our ground-work was well done, my friends. In another forty-eight hours we will have such a strangle-hold on every important center in the country that the government will have to surrender."

WASHINGTON, D.C.

The President's face was drawn, white, ghastly. The three men who had just come into his private study were gravely silent. As the chief executive looked eagerly at their faces, the last vestige of hope appeared to fade from his eyes.

"Well, gentlemen?"

General Barrett, Chief of the M.I.D., cleared his throat. "What news there is, is bad, sir. The attack was such a surprise in all quarters that the Red Sleeves have been almost universally successful. What they have done in ten hours, sir, would take us weeks and weeks to undo, even if we were ready to move at once."

"And we are not?" asked the President.

"Communications are so badly disrupted, sir. Railroad lines have been put out of commission. We will be terribly handicapped in attempting to move large numbers of men with any speed. They have taken towns and cities by surprise—with no resistance offered them. We'll have to gain them back by open fighting—with the enemy well-entrenched. It's going to be a tremendous task, sir."

"And you, Admiral?" the President asked.

Admiral Hewitt, Chief of the Naval Intelligence, tried to make his smile seem reassuring. "We are ready to act on your orders, sir. Attempts were made to take several naval bases but they have all failed to date. Ships and navy planes, sir, are ready to move on any point you say. We can wipe the Red Sleeves out of any of the seaboard cities."

"And kill millions of innocent citizens in the process," said the President bitterly.

"Stern measures may be necessary, sir," said the Admiral. "But, as Barrett says, it will take weeks to fight our way back into a position of control, for as they are forced to give way they will leave a path of destruction behind them."

"And you, Corcoran?"

Corcoran's stiff knee was stretched out before him and his fingers rubbed it nervously. "Nothing to report, sir."

"No word from Vane?"

"None, sir," said Corcoran grimly. "But that doesn't mean much. He can't report by telephone or telegraph."

"Do you know that he reached New York safely?"

Corcoran's lips were caught between his teeth. His eyes wavered from the chief executive's eager, searching look. "The plane that took them to New York was shot down, sir," he said quietly. "However, we have reason to believe that Vane and his men escaped. A devious report from an agent of ours was flown back here about an hour ago. Only the pilot's body was found in the wreckage."

The President passed a hand across his eyes. "I've been trying to think this thing out, gentlemen," he said slowly. "I—I confess I am at a loss to know what the course of wisdom is. If—if I were to step down out of office now—tonight—this thing would end. Wouldn't that be better than all this bloodshed? If it's what the people want...."

His face was tense.

"They *don't* want it, sir!" said Corcoran. "Millions of them are looking to you for leadership in this crisis. If the people wanted this they could have ousted you at the polls. We know, sir, what is behind this! You cannot, you *must* not think of anything but fighting, sir. You are Commander in Chief of the army and navy and every last man in the service is with you. You haven't the *right* to give up, sir, till you have won this fight!"

"But at what a cost, Corcoran! Millions and millions of lives, perhaps."

"May I remind you that you have sworn, sir, to defend the Constitution of the United States! You cannot give up without breaking that oath! You cannot give up until every last drop of blood of every loyal American citizen has been shed to uphold that Constitution. Any other course is unthinkable, sir. This is not a fight to keep *you* in office! It is a fight for the principles upon which this nation was founded!"

Corcoran's voice seemed to ring like a bell in that small office.

Suddenly the President held out his hand to the lame man, and there was light in his eyes once more.

"Thank you, Corcoran," he said, very simply. "Thank you for reminding me."

TIMES SQUARE, NEW YORK CITY:

"Are you going to stand for being ruled by a dictator? Because that's what is happening! A dictator is taking over with the help of gunmen and criminals, and the backing of economic robber barons!"

The speaker was standing on an upturned box, shouting at a great crowd of men and women who stood before him— gathered there to watch the moving electric sign on the Times

Building. Over that sign came news that told of the sweep of the revolution the length and breadth of the nation.

The lights twinkled on and off as the blazing letters moved steadily around the building in a continuous belt.

The crowd stared up at them, seeming bludgeoned by the story that came to life as they watched.

"They tell us they are going to make America a place for Americans!" the speaker shouted. "Yet the blood of Americans is running in the gutters. They have shot down our friends! Did they give us a chance to choose in this matter? No! They have jumped on us like some beast of prey! They haven't given us any choice. Is that American? Is that the freedom for which we stand? We cannot ride our subways! We cannot telephone our families or reach them if they live out of the city! Our banks have closed! America for Americans! Do Americans want a dictator? No! Do we want to be regimented by a one-armed Mussolini drunk with power? No! Let us decide this in an American way. Let them hold a special election if they like! Let them impeach the President if they've got something on him. Let them...."

His voice was drowned out by another voice—a voice coming through huge amplifiers mounted on a truck which had driven up to the outskirts of the crowd:

> "Street meetings are not permitted by order of General Elli-son. You must disperse at once. We have no desire to take life unnecessarily but unless this breaks up at once machine guns which are trained on the square from the surrounding build-ings will be brought into action. Move on! Demonstrations of any kind are not allowed!"

The man on the box raised his voice to an almost hysterica scream: "Are you people going to let them deny you the right of discussion—the right of free speech? Is *that* American? Is *that* what we're headed for? If any of you have one drop of red blood in you, you won't stand for this abuse of your rights! Are you going to...."

In an upper window of a building across the square a man

in a gray uniform rested a high-powered rifle on the window sill. Calmly he squinted along the barrel and then his fingers squeezed the trigger. The man on the box was stopped in the middle of his speech… strangling, choking, his fingers clawing at his throat. Then he toppled over onto the pavement.

The marksman rested the butt of his rifle on the floor. He lit a cigarette and watched the crowd scurrying off like frightened rabbits. Nobody bothered to pick up the man who had spoken so passionately of freedom.

ATLANTA, GEORGIA:

Five miles from the famous State Penitentiary a farmer and his wife sat huddled around their cheap radio set listening to the astounding news. Suddenly their attention was diverted by a strange noise at the door of their house—a sound like a dog scratching for admittance. But it was not the farmer's dog. That animal, a hound, was crouched at his master's feet, hackles on end, teeth bared, yet whining with fright.

The farmer rose quietly, took his shotgun down from a rack on the wall, and went softly over to the door. He opened it. And then he screamed.

Something fell into the room. It was a man, a man naked save where his muscular body was caked with blood and dirt. As he lay, face down on the worn carpet, the farmer and his wife saw evidence of the lash having been laid unmercifully across his back.

"Escaped convict," the horrified woman whispered.

"Get something to put around him," the farmer said grimly. "Convict or no convict, he's mighty close to bein' dead."

They lifted the man onto the bed. With warm water and soap they washed the dirt from his cruel wounds. A cool white sheet covered him. Suddenly the man opened his eyes, eyes still sick with horror. As he saw the kindly faces of the farmer and his wife the man began to sob.

"You made a break from the pen," said the farmer gently.

The man groaned: "I—I'm not a convict. I'm one of the

guards! Maybe the only one left… except the ones that betrayed us! It's—it's the Red Sleeves!

"They had men planted among the guards. Tonight these phony guards turned 'em loose. They got the arsenal. They killed most of the guards—beat 'em until they died. They left me for dead. They—they hung the warden! And now they're heading for Atlanta to join up with the Red Sleeves there. Prisons all over the country… they're turnin' murderers loose to do their work!"

The man closed his eyes. When they tried to force a little corn liquor between his teeth they were clamped tight in death.

NEW YORK CITY:

On the wall of a huge, high-ceilinged room, in that square gray-stone house on Fifth Avenue was a huge map. It was a large scale map of the country. It was studded with tiny electric light bulbs, some shining green, many more shining red. Standing before the map was General Edward Ellison, lower lip jutting out pugnaciously, legs spread apart, a feverish brilliance in his eyes.

He was watching the map, and even as he watched green lights went out to be replaced by red ones.

Sprawling in an armchair was another man in the uniform of the Red Sleeves. It was Lefty Brace, Chief of General Ellison's Intelligence Staff, the man who had laid the ground-work for the rebellion. A cigarette dangled between his lips, and his manner was one of complete contentment.

"Well, General, how do you like the look of things?"

The ever-present frown split Ellison's forehead. He pointed a bony finger at the map. "We have failed in several critical spots," he said, in his snarling voice, as he indicated one or two green-burning bulbs. "The power plant at Niagara; the naval base at San Diego; the White House; the government airport at Washington; a dozen others!"

Brace laughed good-naturedly. "Twelve hours, General. We have been under way twelve hours and we have only failed in a few places. Wait till this time tomorrow!"

Ellison turned to fix his glowing eyes on his subordinate.

"If we hadn't been forced to strike ahead of schedule, there'd have been no failures at all!"

There was a whip-lash to his voice. He scowled. His eyes were pinpoints of angry light.

Brace shrugged. "Not my fault, General! But it looks to me as if what we failed to take by force we'll acquire by pressure. I have arranged safe conduct for myself for a conference with the powers that be here in the city—eight o'clock this morning. One hour after that we will have complete control of New York. And the same plan will work in other cities all over the country. We've got 'em by the throat, General, and we aren't going to let go." A shrewd, half amused light flickered in Brace's shifty eyes. "In forty-eight hours you will be in the White House!"

The General squared his shoulders; his eyes glowed under the bushy eyebrows.

"It is the people's will," he said solemnly.

CHAPTER XIII

BATTLE IN 9B

DOMINICK VANE STOOD in the tiny vestibule of the apartment house on West End Avenue, his pencil torch playing over the names on the bell board. Opposite 9B was a woman's name—*Miss Kay Garvin.*

Vane dropped the cigarette he had been smoking on the tile floor and crushed it out under his heel. A woman! This girl was probably some friend of Angela's—someone in whom she had confided. And yet he was unwilling to risk his personal safety on this guess.

From the inside pocket of his coat Dominick produced a thin leather case. It contained some slender, shining steel tools and after a quick look up and down the Avenue, he stepped back into the vestibule and went carefully to work on the door lock. Five minutes later he had mastered it and he slipped quietly into the inner hall.

There was apparently no one on duty there, and he saw a moment later that there was an automatic elevator. If there *was* a night man he was probably asleep in the basement. Dominick stepped into the elevator and pressed the button which would take him up to the ninth floor. The building was dead quiet. It was nearly three in the morning and the tenants were either in bed or keeping pretty quiet.

There were only four apartments on each floor and 9B was directly opposite the elevator doors as he stepped off. In a little brass frame on the door was a calling card which repeated that the tenant was *Miss Kay Garvin.* Vane hesitated only a second. If this Garvin woman was a friend of Angela's he would be readily admitted. If she was not, any attempt of his to open the door with his tools might have unpredictable results. He must ring the door bell and trust to luck. He slipped his gun out of the holster under his arm and dropped it into his coat pocket, keeping his right hand over it. With his left he rang the bell.

There was delay and then he heard a woman's voice say quietly: "Who is it?"

"A friend," said Dominick Vane softly.

There was a moment's hesitation and then the door opened a crack and he saw Miss Kay Garvin. Instantly his senses warned him that this woman was not a friend of Angela's. She was a platinum blonde. Scarlet fingernails gripped the edge of the door. Her mouth was a red gash in chalk. And Dominick thought he had never seen such sheer terror as was mirrored in the dark violet eyes.

"I… I don't know you," said Kay Garvin. Her voice shook a little.

Dominick had inserted his foot in the door opening, but he did not try to force his way in. "I must talk to you at once, Miss Garvin. It is vitally important. I am a government agent."

The girl suddenly tried to slam the door, but Dominick's shoulder was against it. "I simply want to talk to you, Miss Garvin," he said. "I promise you I want nothing more than that. Are you alone?"

"Yes," she whispered. "But if I let you in they'll… they'll kill me!"

"They?" asked Dominick. As he spoke he forced his way into the apartment and closed the door behind him. The girl stood with her back to the wall. She had raised a bright green chiffon handkerchief to her lips as if to stifle a scream.

"What do you want to bother me for?" the girl asked. "I haven't done anything—I swear it. You can't do anything to me."

Beyond the little foyer Dominick could see the living room of the apartment, dimly lit.

"Can't we go in there, sit down, and talk things over quietly?" he said.

"If he comes—" the girl started, and then checked herself.

VERY GENTLY Dominick took her arm and led her into the living room. "If anybody comes who might object to my presence," he said, "you have nothing to worry about. These are war times or the equivalent. I don't need a warrant to force my way in here."

Kay Garvin sat on the edge of a couch, her scarlet lips caught between her teeth. "What do you want of me?" she asked.

"Where is Angela Dawson?" Dominick asked.

A look of bewilderment mingled with relief flashed across her face. "I never heard of her," she said. Dominick's eyes, hard and cold, bored into hers and he had a feeling that she was speaking the truth.

"You don't know Angela Dawson?"

"No. I never heard of her."

"That's odd," said Dominick quietly, "because, in a way, she sent me to you."

"She sent you…?"

Dominick took a package of cigarettes from his pocket, passed it to the girl who shook her head in silence. He selected one for himself, lit it, and watched the smoke curl up toward the ceiling before he spoke.

"Never heard of H.R. Dawson?" he asked.

"He—he's a banker, or something, isn't he?"

"Or something," said Dominick. He leaned forward. "I'm going to be frank with you, Miss Garvin. I'm looking for Dawson and his ward, Miss Angela Dawson. In Dawson's house I found your address. It suggested to me that you might know something about their whereabouts." All the time he talked Vane sensed that the girl's tension was relaxing. It was as if she were tremendously relieved by his line of questioning. It bothered him. He was missing the opening that the girl's first terror had afforded him.

"I can't imagine what my address would be doing in the Dawson house," said the girl quite calmly. And then, as she said it, her eyes suddenly dilated. Dominick knew that she had guessed in that moment what the address was doing there. At the same moment he saw the pipe.

It lay in a silver-plated ash tray on the little coffee table not a foot from where he sat. It was a well-charred briar and the end of the stem was bitten through, as though the owner had constantly gripped it very tightly between strong teeth. The girl saw the direction of his glance and the chiffon handkerchief was suddenly tightly entwined around the vivid red-tipped fingers.

"You don't live here alone?" said Dominick.

"Oh, I do! Indeed I do!" she said eagerly. "That... that pipe. It belongs to a friend of mine. He... he left it here by mistake."

DOMINICK SMILED, thin-lipped. "When I came in," he said, "you said 'if I let you in they'll kill me!' Who were you referring to, Miss Garvin?"

"Why... why the Red Sleeves! They would kill me for having a government agent here in my place."

"Later you said, 'If *he* comes...' Who were you talking about, Miss Garvin?" Dominick's tone was implacable.

"Oh—let me alone!" It was a cry of despair. "There's nothing I can tell you—nothing I can do to help you! Can't you see that's the truth?"

"I see that you're in mortal terror of something, Miss Garvin—of *someone*. Who is it?"

She leaned forward suddenly, one white hand clutching at his coat sleeve. "All right... I lied to you!" Her words began to come out in a torrent of eagerness. "I have a sweetheart. He's terribly jealous. If he were to come here and find you he wouldn't believe... he wouldn't believe that you are a government agent. He'd kill me."

"What's his name?" said Dominick.

"Oh why don't you go!"

"What is the man's name?" said Dominick grimly. "Don't you see, Miss Garvin, it may have been *his* address that I found in the Dawson house."

"It *was*," cried the girl. "It was his address. I don't know the Dawsons. I told you that... I...."

And then she smothered a hysterical sob and sat rigid as a stone image. There was the sound of a key turning in the front door lock!

Dominick had just time to get up from his chair before the figure of a man in the gray uniform of the Red Sleeves came into the room. It was Moxelli.

"So, my sweet," he snarled, "you couldn't wait for me to be gone before you had another man up here! I told you what I'd do if you pulled anything like that." Then he swung around and for the first time recognized the girl's caller.

"Vane!"

THINGS HAPPENED very quickly in the next ten seconds. Moxelli snatched his gun from the holster at his side. Dominick had no time to swing his own gun into action, and what he did was purely instinctive—the result of long experience in making hair-trigger decisions. He launched a savage kick at Moxelli's gun hand. The gun went off, but at the same time spun out of Moxelli's hand. Then they closed.

Dominick was an expert at rough and tumble fighting, but in the first seconds of that encounter he realized that Moxelli, too, knew all the tricks. They fought silently. Dominick drove a sharp right to Moxelli's jaw, but the fat man did not seem to feel it. His knee came up—the nails of his left hand raked the flesh of Dominick's cheek—and then he drove a blow to the agent's mid-section that had Dominick's knees sagging. There were muscles of steel under those layers of flabby fat. Moxelli's eyes burned with fury.

At long range Dominick realized he had the best of it. His

reach was longer and his boxing science was tops. He raked a
left, and a right, and a left again to Moxelli's head; and then the
big man closed with a rush, trying to get those powerful arms
around Dominick, kicking, trying to get in that blow with his
knee which would end the fight. Dominick backed away, knif-
ing through the big man's guard with stinging blows to the face.
Moxelli was bleeding, breathing hard, but he had lost none of
his steam. And then Dominick tripped over a chair and Moxelli
was on him, crushing him, his teeth bestially sunk into the flesh
of Dominick's neck.

Other things were happening which Dominick was aware of
as he fought. Kay Garvin had picked up Moxelli's gun and was
standing over them. Desperately, Dominick realized that if he
exposed himself long enough she would probably shoot him.
And so he twisted and writhed in Moxelli's powerful grip and
they rolled over and over.

And men were hammering at the door! Shouting Moxelli's
name, asking him if he was all right! The gun shot must have
attracted some of the Red Sleeve leader's henchmen. Then above
the din he heard Kay Garvin's voice.

"Kill him, Mr. Vane! Kill him! I'll hold the others off!" It was
a hysterical scream. And she rushed out into the foyer with
the gun. "Get away from the door or I'm shooting!" Dominick
heard her cry.

Somehow new strength flowed into Dominick's system as he
realized he had an ally. The girl had cast her lot with him—stak-
ing her life on his chance of victory. For if Moxelli got him he
would certainly kill her for her treachery.

He was on his feet now. Moxelli came in again and Dominck's
right caught him squarely on the mouth. For a moment Moxelli
swayed on his feet, spitting out broken teeth. And in that
moment of hesitation Dominick had him. His right hand closed
over the iron poker of the fire set that stood in a little rack close
by. Before Moxelli could raise weary arms to defend himself
Dominick brought the poker down with savage force over his

skull. As Moxelli crumpled there was a roar of gun fire from the foyer.

Dominick sprang over Moxelli's body to the hall. Kay Garvin lay there, the front of her negligée wet with a rapidly-spreading circle of crimson. Dominick knelt beside her. The assault on the door had begun again.

"Quick! Fire escape…" the girl whispered.

"I can't leave you," he said sharply.

But there was no point in staying. Kay Garvin died there in his arms.

CHAPTER XIV

MANHATTAN ISOLATED

A BEWILDERED CITY awoke the next morning to the second day of the Red Sleeve revolution. It was hard for the average citizen of the great metropolis to assimilate what had happened. Yet there was evidence enough to aid the slow percolating of the truth into his mind. His morning paper was there—but different. It spoke of the revolutionists in heroic terms. It spoke in high-flown, patriotic terms of the "Cause"; of "America For Americans"; of "The Spirit of Our Forefathers"! It told of "treacherous and double-crossing city officials" fleeing the city.

Mr. Average Citizen was faced with a curious situation. Obviously he would not go to work today. Subways, buses, taxis, were commandeered, some by the revolutionists, some by the battered police and military forces. Only men employed at certain vital points concerned with the necessities of civilization found their way to work. Telephone service was completely disrupted.

The Red Sleeves had taken no chances on holding telephone exchanges. They had destroyed the service. The twisted masses of telephone cables under the city streets had been hacked to pieces. But over the radio came news flashes and a constant stream of propaganda; nothing else. The usual and familiar broadcasters were not at the microphones. Instead, agents of the Red Sleeves poured out sympathetic facts about the revolution: It was rumored from Washington that the President had met his death in the first hours of the revolution. It was rumored that there was wholesale mutiny in both army and navy. Red

Sleeve officials promised that order would be restored within a week and that men of high caliber would take over the offices of government. Citizens were urged to throw their weight on the side of Right! To give moral and physical support to those sons of the early Americans who were out to crush oppressors of the people! There were speeches about General Ellison, "that great American hero who had given his arm 'to make the world safe for democracy' in 1917 and is now waging this war within the country to place us back on that level of high ideals, of Americanism, that our forefathers visioned for us!"

Then General Ellison came to the microphone. "We are fighting," he said, "to drive political rats and greedy men of wealth out of high places and supplant them with *Americans!*"

But Mr. Average Citizen was a little too bewildered to take in anything but cold facts. There was blood in the streets; transportation and communication systems were crippled; what about food? What about water supply? People who had cars considered the possibility of taking their worldly goods and leaving town for the comparative safety of scarcely-populated rural centers. Those who tried found the Island of Manhattan ringed with steel. Red Sleeves held the bridges, the tubes, the ferries.

Where were the police? Where were the military from Governors Island? Where were the National Guard and the emergency organizations? In the early hours of the second day neither blue nor khaki was visible anywhere in that great city. What was the answer? Were there no forces left loyal to the government? Had the Red Sleeves swept everything in front of them in the short space of twelve hours? It was incredible to Mr. Average Citizen.

THE ANSWER lay in one of the strangest gatherings that a country had ever seen—a gathering in the offices of the Mayor at City Hall on lower Broadway.

Men sat around a table, faces grim, listening to the most extraordinary ultimatum that was ever delivered to men in power. The Mayor was there; the police commissioner and his chief; General Trent, in command of the first army at Governors Island; and commanders of National Guard and Reserve Officers units. And one other man was there—a man in the gray shirt and scarlet arm bands of the Red Sleeves. He was short, stocky, red-haired, with the quick shifting eyes of a fighter, and there was a mocking smile on his lips as he looked scornfully at the men around the table.

"This is a moment, gentlemen, for which I have waited a very long time," he said. There was a knifelike, insulting edge to his voice.

"We are waiting to hear what you have to say, Mr. Brace," said the Mayor quietly.

"Oh, I've got plenty to say, Mr. Mayor," drawled Lefty Brace. "I have come here, as a matter of fact, to issue *orders!*" And his eyes blazed.

General Trent sprang to his feet and his fingers hovered close to the revolver he was carrying in a holster on his hip.

"Sit down!" Brace's voice cracked like a pistol shot. "I'm doing the talking, General Trent, and you'll do well to listen! When I'm through it will be your turn! I have come here alone under your guarantee of protection. If you should be tempted to use that gun on me, General, you would have the lives of millions of citizens on your conscience!"

Trent sat down, his jaws clamped together, his face white.

"We're listening, Mr. Brace," said the Mayor in a harsh voice.

Brace looked around the room, smiling. He was taking full satisfaction in this moment of power. "The orders I have come to issue are these, gentlemen. There must be no military movement against the Red Sleeves in New York. The police must withdraw from their positions and throw down their arms. The National Guard units must disband!" He said it all very calmly.

Somebody laughed, a jangling, high-tensioned laugh.

"And if we refuse these absurd demands, Mr. Brace?" said General Trent.

"It is not our purpose, General, to take life unnecessarily. But

if our hand is forced we will kill *millions* to gain our objective—which in this instance is control of New York!"

"Are you trying to tell us," said General Trent slowly, "that you believe you have a strong enough force of men here in New York to defeat the combined forces of the army, the navy, the police, and the reserve units, Mr. Brace? Because if you are, you are talking lunacy!"

"I am making no such claim, General," said Lefty Brace suavely. "But what I am claiming is, that unless you withdraw *all* your forces at once we are in a position to wipe out almost completely the entire civilian population of the city. Let me point out just what the situation is—in case you are not aware of it."

"Go on, Mr. Brace," said the general grimly.

BRACE SMILED his crooked little smile of triumph. "In less than twenty minutes from the time of a given signal, General," he said, "we can snap off New York's water supply. The Croton Dam is in our hands. You might be able to fight off our men, but you could not fight off the charge of dynamite which would blow it to hell before they were defeated. Further up State we are prepared to destroy aqueducts or put disease germs in the water. The freight yards and provision warehouses of the city are in our hands. They would meet with the same fate. We hold every single bridge and tunnel leading out of the city. In twenty minutes after your refusal to obey our orders, general, those bridges and tunnels would be nothing more than a mass of twisted iron and stone! Without food and water people cannot live, General. And without bridges and tunnels they cannot leave to find it elsewhere. And if you believe this is a high-sounding threat, a boast rather than fact, call in your engineers and I will prove my familiarity with the situation by telling them exactly the spots where our high explosives are placed. This is not a gag, gentlemen—*it is fact!*"

"And what about your own men if you destroy sources of food and water?"

Brace smiled. "Do you imagine that if we were so well prepared to strike this blow, we have not prepared for such a contingency. No, gentlemen, you have the manpower but we have the strategic jump on you. In short, gentlemen, this is a very excellent case of blackmail and you've got to *pay our price!* And our price is the withdrawal of your armed forces at once."

There was a prolonged silence in the room. Then General Trent spoke:

"How long will you give us to come to a decision, Mr. Brace?"

Brace glanced at his wrist-watch and a very faint smile curled his lips. "I'll give you exactly one hour," he said.

At that moment the door of the Mayor's office opened and a haggard secretary stepped in.

"Mr. Dominick Vane," she announced.

Vane, his clothes rumpled and dirty, his face gray and streaked with dust, came in. He was the picture of infinite weariness, and only the intense brightness of his eyes gave hint to the vitality that lay beneath the surface. He started to speak, and then his eyes rested on Brace and his whole figure stiffened as, if from a jolt of electricity.

"Brace!" His gun was out of his pocket in a flash. It was General Trent who sprang up and seized his arm. Lefty Brace smiled that mocking, twisted smile of his.

"Well," he drawled, "If it isn't our hero from Washington. What a situation! All ready for fireworks and he can't set them off."

"Brace is here under a guarantee of protection and a safe-conduct pass from us," said Trent harshly.

Dominick wrenched his arm free and his gun was pointed steadily at the Red Sleeve leader. "I don't give a damn about safe-conduct passes," he snapped. "This man holds the whole key to our problem in the palm of his hand! Where is Dawson, Brace?"

"Little boys must learn to keep their tempers," said Brace mockingly. "You really don't think I'd answer any questions of that sort, do you?"

"You're going to answer whether you like it or not," said Dominick grimly. "You're going to tell me where Dawson is. And you're going to tell me what's become of his ward, Miss Angela, and his nephew Philip Jaxon."

"So touching, all this," said Brace. "We now have the heart interest. What has become of the heroine? Dear, dear Mr. Vane, a smart man like you ought to be able to find out a thing like that."

SOMEHOW DOMINICK managed to jerk himself away from Trent and the police commissioner who was standing on the other side of him. His left fist shot out and caught Brace flush on the mouth. The Red Sleeve staggered back against the Mayor's desk and his hand was streaked with crimson as he brought it away from his lips. The general and the commissioner had seized Vane and were holding him tightly now.

"Get this straight, Vane," said the general grimly. "This man holds the safety of millions of citizens in his hands."

Lefty Brace straightened up and there was a glow of murderous fury in his close-set eyes. "For that, Dominick Vane, I'll cut your heart out!" he said, very slowly, his voice deadly cold. He turned to the others. "There is no need for me to stay here any longer, gentlemen. If you have not issued your orders for the withdrawal of troops in accordance with our demands within one hour, we will take it that you refuse to comply with our wishes and act accordingly! Good day." He stalked toward the office door.

"You can't let him go!" Dominick cried. "Why, damn it, he can be made to tell us all we need to know! Hold him! Defy these rats! Knowing what Brace knows we can wipe 'em out in twenty-four hours. I don't know what kind of a bluff he's pulling on you, but don't let him get away with it. *You can't let him go!*"

General Trent tugged savagely at his gray mustache. "God help me," he said bitterly, "I can't take the responsibility."

"Goodbye, Mr. Dominick Vane," said Brace, at the door. "You need have no fear about seeing me again. I shall make a personal point of it!" And he was gone.

For a moment Dominick stood staring at the door, his body shaken by a wild, impotent fury. Then very suddenly he sank into a chair and covered his face with his hands. No one spoke. The minds and hearts of all those men must have been dark with despair at that moment. Finally Dominick looked up.

"You will have to forgive me, gentlemen, if I lost control for a moment or two," he said, in a low voice. "You see, in Washington we feel that the only quick way to smash this rebellion is by getting evidence of the real purpose behind it. Brace knows everything! To see him walk out of here unmolested was just too much!"

"Tough on all of us," said General Trent gruffly.

"And only an hour ago I had another big-shot in my hands

and had to let him slip through my fingers, too," said Dominick. He told them about his encounter with Moxelli.

"You killed him?" Trent asked.

Dominick shrugged. "I don't know. I doubt it. It was only a glancing blow I struck him. I couldn't wait to make certain because a dozen of his men were breaking into the apartment. I just got down the fire escape and away by the skin of my teeth. What did Brace want here?"

"Plenty," said the General grimly. And he outlined the Red Sleeve demands.

"What are you going to do?" Dominick asked.

The general tugged fiercely at his mustache. "What *can* we do? Personally I can't take the responsibility of defying them. There are millions of innocent and loyal citizens here in New York. Their lives would be too great a price to pay for victory! New York is only one center of the revolt. If we were to fight back and they carried out their threats... well, millions of people all over the country would swing to their side out of fear for their lives. I am going to withdraw my troops and await orders from the President. The responsibility must rest with him."

"I feel the same way," said the police commissioner gravely.

The Mayor nodded. "There is no alternative left us, gentlemen, but to give in to these demands—for the time being, at least. None of us, I think, wishes to be responsible for mass murder!"

DOMINICK LEFT the council chamber with General Trent. The tough old warrior's face was black as a thunder cloud. Retreat and submission went as strongly against the grain with him as it did with Dominick Vane. Outside the Mayor's office they paused.

"Well, I suppose we go our own way, General," said Dominick. "I have a job to do that is not affected by this ultimatum."

"I want to talk to you before you go," the general said. "There's an empty office down the line here." He took Dominick's arm and led him along the corridor. Once in the empty office the general began to storm the floor like a caged animal.

"I know how you felt in there, Vane," he rapped. "You felt as if we were all quitters. Well—I for one am not. But we've got to tread cautiously—very cautiously."

"You mean...?"

"I mean I know all about you, Vane. Know what confidence the President has in you and the job he's given you. I had orders to coöperate with you in every way. But I couldn't hold Brace. You see that."

"Yes, I see that," said Dominick grimly.

The general continued to pace the floor. "If we were dealing with an alien enemy, Vane, it would be a different story," he said. "There'd be no compromise then. We'd blockade the city—bring the fleet into the harbor—let 'em die in their own trap! But this—well, a man can't deal with it in the same way."

"I know."

The general stopped his pacing and stared thoughtfully at Dominick. "You fellows believe there is concrete evidence which would prove that Dawson and other financiers are back of this thing?"

Dominick nodded. "And we believe further, sir, that if that evidence were placed before the sincere members of the Red Sleeve organization that they would turn against their leaders and the back of the revolution would be broken."

"How do you propose to go about getting that evidence?" the general asked.

Dominick lit a cigarette and inhaled deeply on it. "Somewhere there is a secret headquarters where Dawson and his friends are hiding out," he said. "If I can find them the evidence I need will probably be close at hand."

"Any clues?"

"None," said Dominick darkly. "Moxelli could have told me if I'd had a chance to make him talk. Brace could have told us. But with those chances gone, sir, I feel pretty well baffled."

The general looked thoughtfully out the window. "I don't pretend to be an expert on intelligence work," he said. "But I do know this. In war-time a spy who operates *outside* the enemy ranks very seldom gets any information worth having. Without undercover men in the enemy ranks, your spy system breaks down entirely."

Dominick's hard cold eyes were fixed intently on the general's face, but he said nothing.

"One of the main reasons for the Red Sleeve success in these first hours," said the soldier, "is the fact that we haven't got one shred of information coming to us from the inside. We are handicapped in a military way—an army without eyes cannot fight an enemy with eyes. And it's undercover men in the enemy ranks that are the eyes of an army."

"And how do we go about placing undercover men in their ranks?" Dominick asked. There was a curious, flat quality to his voice because he knew the answer to his own question. He was thinking far ahead.

The general looked down at the gnarled knuckles of his right hand. "They are enlisting recruits to the cause already," he said quietly. "Half a dozen recruiting stations have been set up here in the city."

Neither man spoke for a moment, and then their eyes me; in a long, steady stare. "Of course you're dead right, General," said Dominick at last. "Until we have men on the inside who can anticipate their next moves they'll go on winning by sheer surprise."

"Exactly."

Dominick stood up and held out his hand. "I'm glad I had this chat with you, sir. I—I think we can do something about this."

"If you do," said the general, "try to arrange some method of keeping me in touch." They shook hands warmly. "Good luck, Vane."

"Thank you, sir," said Dominick grimly. "I have a hunch I'm going to need it."

CHAPTER XV

TO THE PEOPLE

IN A QUIET corner of a reading room of the Public Library Dominick met his three assistants, Harbold, Ives and Dugan. The three men had very little to report to their chief that he did not already know or guess! The city was in the hands of the revolutionists... it meant death to open your mouth against the Cause... food was being doled out on a ration basis.

Then Dominick told them of his own adventures, and of his plans. "I'm not issuing orders," he said quietly. "Spy work is volunteer work."

"Naturally we're for it," said Johnny Harbold quickly. "But I'm thinking about you, Nick. You're known. It's suicide for you to attempt this job. Dugan and Ives and I can swing it—report to you. But you stay out of it."

Dominick laughed, a short, clipped laugh. "I'd be fit for a psychopathic ward in twenty-four hours... just waiting for you guys to turn something up," he said. "Besides, the only people who know me by sight are Brace, Moxelli and Dawson and his crowd. I'm not apt to get next to them in a hurry. No, Johnny, we're all going to take a crack at this. One or more of us may get somewhere."

"I think it's crazy, Nick, for you," said Harbold stubbornly.

"Which may be one reason why I might succeed," said Dominick. "About reports... Pass on any news you may pick up to Trent. We'll have to perfect some means of communication with him later. Until we do we can use this place for meetings and for a message depot. We're not apt to be bothered here." He turned and looked at the bookshelves behind him. A faint smile twisted his lips. *"The Decline and Fall of the Roman Empire!* I doubt if anyone will be reading that in these times. If any of you have any information to pass on to the rest of us, write it somewhere in the margins of this book—volume two. Try to keep in touch as often as possible. You're to go about this thing in your own way. I don't care how you get on the inside—*but get there!* That's all."

Dugan and Ives went off, but red-headed Johnny Harbold lingered behind. "Listen, Dominick," he said gravely, "you're not kidding me about the risk you'll be running trying to muscle into this outfit. You're a pretty important guy in the scheme of things."

"Johnny, I never did my fighting from behind a desk. I've been ordered to do a job and I'm going to do it. This seems the best way of accomplishing our objective and so this is the way we're going to work it."

"I've seen some pretty unpleasant things in the last few hours," said Harbold gravely. "I saw a guy shot down in cold blood in Times Square for speaking against the Cause. They're dealing brutally with all loyalists on the basis that the tougher they are now the less trouble they'll have later. You can stumble over dead sympathizers of the government almost anywhere you turn. And the Red Sleeves won't be nice to the spies they catch. There's too much at stake. You would be fair game for any of them! Active Chief of the Intelligence Service! The man who blows your brains out will rate plenty high!"

Dominick's lips relaxed in a faint smile. "You aren't trying to scare me, are you, Johnny?"

For a minute Johnny Harbold looked at his chief in silence. "It looks like I'm wasting quite a lot of time," he drawled. "So long, Dominick."

"Good hunting," said Dominick.

WASHINGTON, D.C.

The President's Study.

"That's the way the situation stands, sir. General Trent is waiting for your orders." It was a young man in the uniform of an army flier who stood before the Chief Executive's desk. He had just arrived from the Army Headquarters at Governors Island with news of the Red Sleeve ultimatum.

The President gazed at Corcoran who, with Hewitt and Barrett, had gathered to hear this report. Suddenly he brought his clenched fist down on his desk. "We never realize in times of peace how vitally important the normal means of communication are! I should be able to call Trent on the phone and talk things over with him. It's like being handcuffed in front of an expert boxer! One not only in front, but on all sides of us— between us and our sources of information and our weapons. This is checkmate, gentlemen! If we attack we alienate millions of supporters. If we don't attack, we're beaten. They have probably made this same play all over the country. The reports will be coming in soon and there isn't anything we can do!"

"If the people could be informed of your situation, Mr. President," said General Barrett. "If they could be told that your hand is forced and that you *have* to fight, it would make a tremendous difference in their morale."

"And how are we to get such information to the people, General?" the President demanded. "They have taken over the newspapers. With one or two minor exceptions all are in their hands. They control the radio stations. How are we to broadcast?"

Corcoran leaned forward in his chair. "There might be a way, Mr. President," he said slowly, "—a spectacular and effective way." He turned to the other two men. "How many planes can we get our hands on in the next eight hours, gentlemen?"

General Barrett thought for a moment. "Perhaps three hundred or more army, naval and commercial planes could be mustered into service in that time."

"Good," snapped Corcoran. "This is my suggestion, Mr. President. That we have this great armada of planes fly over New York

City. The Red Sleeves have a few fighting planes, we know, but not enough to endanger such a fleet."

"And the purpose of this maneuver, Corcoran?"

"We can't drop bombs on the city, sir," said Corcoran, "but there's nothing to prevent our dropping information. It is my suggestion that the government printing presses be put to work at once and that a statement of the situation, signed by you, be drawn up. Explain the Red Sleeve ultimatum. Tell the citizens that as President you cannot give up without a fight. Your hand has been forced and that unless the Red Sleeves withdraw from their position in three days you will have to bring army, navy and flying corps to bear on them and wipe them out, no matter what the cost in life and property. Tell them that they can avert such an eventuality by turning against the revolutionists. We could drop millions of copies of such a proclamation so that in the long run everyone would be bound to know about it. The sight of those planes would encourage people… make them realize that we are ready, that you are still in the saddle, and that we mean business!"

"Corcoran, it is a brilliant idea!" said the President. "We *could* reach almost everyone that way. Copies will be in the hands of the people all over the city before the Red Sleeves can do anything about it!"

"Precisely, sir."

"But what happens, Corcoran, if the Red Sleeves stand pat—refuse to move out—carry through the threats they made to General Trent?" asked the President.

"Then, sir, we attack. We'll wipe them off the face of the earth. Trent can cut off New York by land with his troops. The fleet can move into the harbor. Planes overhead. We can wipe out every Red Sleeve within the city boundaries."

"And a million others at the same time."

"That is something you will have to face, sir. If we show we mean business by handling this New York situation with an iron fist, we may not face resistance anywhere else."

The President looked steadily before him. "We'll go ahead and distribute the proclamations," he said and his gaze shifted to Corcoran. "You can't ask me to give the order to wipe out New York City. I couldn't do it, Mr. Corcoran, nor—if you think—could you. There *must* be some other way."

THEY CAME, like the humming of a million bees in the distance—like the droning of some huge dynamo. First they were a blot on the distant blue horizon, then a huge, dark cloud, and then suddenly, in awesome array they were over the city, a great roaring, mechanical blanket that seemed at times to blot out the sun. Three hundred or more planes flying in elaborate geometrical formation. If the Red Sleeves had fighting planes they did not appear. It would have been futile to offer resistance to this enormous fleet.

Already paralyzed by the brutal bewilderment of the events of the past days, the city was completely stunned by this new show of force.

At first there was panic in the streets below. People rushed out of their houses to stare up, pale and trembling at what they thought must be an attacking squadron that would demolish the city before they could scurry to places of safety. But there were no bombs.

Around the city they wheeled, the roar from those hundreds of motors deafening, terrifying. Out of every house people came to stare up at the heavens. Lower and lower the planes flew until it seemed they were in danger of fatal collision with some of the taller buildings. And then, suddenly, the air was white—a sudden storm of gargantuan flakes of snow. Paper, tons and tons of floating white piper, came drifting down into the canyons that were the city streets.

The imagination of a populace, raised to a hysterical pitch by what had gone before, could easily envision its dreadful situation if the planes had dropped bombs, not paper.

Round and round over the city they flew, leaving behind their heavy clouds of proclamations. There could not have been a hundred who did not have the chance to pick up one of those slips of paper. And then the planes roared away south again, leaving the people of New York with the pounding of motors in their ears and the pounding of fear in their hearts as they read the President's Proclamation:

TO THE PEOPLE OF THE CITY OF NEW YORK:

The Red Sleeves have handed down an ultimatum to the Government of the United States.

They have ordered the Government to withdraw its troops, its police, its national guard units. To offer no resistance to the revolutionary movement.

If we fail to obey this order they threaten to cut off the city's water supply, its food supply, its means of communication. To spread disease and death that will wipe out the city's population.

The Government has complied with these demands. BUT WILL DO SO ONLY FOR A PERIOD OF THREE DAYS.

In that time it is hoped the Red Sleeve leaders will reconsider their purpose. At the end of three days the Government will move to take the city from their control.

Our hand has been forced. In three days, army, navy and all other Government forces will attack.

The President has sworn to uphold the Constitution and he will do so with men and guns!

Unless the Red Sleeves have relinquished their hold on the city by Saturday morning the Government strikes!

THE PRESIDENT

The light of battle was in General Trent's eyes as he looked up from his desk to confront Dominick Vane. The old warrior's jaws seemed a little squarer, his mouth a little grimmer. He looked like a man who had just been reprieved from the death house.

"Well, Mr. Vane, how do you like our government now?" he cried.

Dominick moistened his lips. His face was pinched, haggard. "I never saw anything like it," he said a little hoarsely. "Those planes were magnificent… and they were terrible. An air force of that size could turn this city into a shambles in half an hour!"

"And *will!*" snapped the general. "Unless these Red-Sleeved vermin back down we'll blow them to hallelujah. I'd like to see Mr. Brace's face now."

"It's—it's not a bluff, sir, this proclamation?" Dominick asked.

"Bluff! *Bluff!* Look out the window, Mr. Vane. Do you see that smoke on the horizon? That's smoke from cruisers and destroyers that are steaming into the harbor. Their guns will be trained on the city for the next three days—waiting!"

Dominick sat silent, his eyes almost closed. He was thinking of the faces he had seen as he made his way to the general's headquarters… faces haunted by fear, and doubt; the faces of people who had struggled all their lives for peace and security and found themselves suddenly caught between the jaws of two fighting machines. He had heard snatches of hushed, frightened talk. He thought he knew the temper of these people. They had lost sight of causes and rights and wrongs. They were thinking of their homes and their loved ones, about to be wiped off the face of the earth unless one of two relentless forces gave in. Dominick knew he would never forget the sight of these faces tortured with the thought of the three-day ultimatum—that would be Saturday—to live or die, yet without the volition to choose.

"I've been proud of my country before," the general was saying. "I was proud when I saw the doughboys marching in the streets of Paris; I was proud when I saw them stand up under fire during their first engagement at the front. But when I read that proclamation and knew that we had men in authority with nerve enough to fight this thing out, then I was really proud."

"But, General Trent, we will be killing our own people!"

"That's war!" said the general. "The innocent must suffer with the guilty!" And then the general cleared his throat. "There is a letter here for you, Vane, from Washington. From the President!"

Vane took the letter and ripped it open. He read:

My dear Dominick Vane:
By now you have read my proclamation to the people of the City of New York. It has been written and delivered with

a heavy heart. You know what this means. I cannot write the words which would describe what will happen if we are forced to act. It is too horrible to contemplate. There is only one hope left me, Mr. Vane, and it is bound up in you.

You said in my office you believed you could get proof of the duplicity of the Red Sleeve leaders. If that can still be done we might yet avoid this catastrophe. You have only three days. I know how hopeless it is—and yet I refuse to give up hope until you have failed. I know you will do whatever is humanly possible for a man to do.

And I want you to know that during every waking moment I shall be praying for you. I have prayed for wisdom in making the decision I have made. But my most earnest pleading is that I will never have to give that order to attack on Saturday morning. And it would seem, Mr. Vane, that you must be the instrument of God if my prayer is to be answered.

God keep and guide you,
The President of the United States.

Very slowly Dominick folded the letter and slipped it into his pocket. That was another face he would never forget—the strong face of that suffering man in the White House.

"The President still hopes the clash can be averted," he told Trent. "He's counting on me to gather the evidence that will do the trick."

"Not a chance, Mr. Vane. You couldn't do that job in three weeks—let alone three days."

"I'm going to try," said Dominick. "What are your plans, General?"

"We're already moving to surround the city," Trent told him. "We'll have 'em shut in here like flies in a bottle. They've got the city shut off now, but we'll spread a wider circle and then move in and crush 'em."

"Will no effort be made to get non-combatants out of the city?"

"An *effort* will be made," said Trent grimly. "We shall try to retake bridges and tubes without destroying them. If we succeed there will be an avenue of escape. But I doubt we'll succeed. The Red Sleeves will blow up those places to keep us out of the city."

Dominick drew a deep breath, and his lips were drawn thin. "Goodbye, General," he said quietly. "You won't see me again till I've won—or lost."

CHAPTER XVI

RECRUIT

GENERAL EDWARD ELLISON stood with his back to the mantelpiece in the library of the stone house on Fifth Avenue from whence the Red Sleeve orders for the whole country were issued. Crumpled savagely into a ball in his one, talonlike hand was a copy of the President's proclamation. Three men stood facing him at attention. In a far corner of the room Lefty Brace sat on the arm of a chair, cigarette dangling between his lips, watching the general with a thoughtful frown.

"Your orders, gentlemen," the general snapped. His lower lip jutted out in that peculiar, pugnacious fashion, and his eyes burned bright beneath the frowning brows. "You will convey to all divisional commanders orders to prepare for a gas attack. See that our men are equipped. Have our chemical experts at their posts twenty-four hours a day, ready to act at a moment's notice."

"Yes, sir."

"I have special orders for the men at the detonators controlling the explosives planted at all bridges, tunnels, water-works and other places. You know exactly where they are all posted, Macklyn?"

"Yes, sir."

"I want extra men at those posts. And I want it understood that if they are attacked or molested at any time they are to set off the explosives without waiting for orders! You understand? We cannot afford to lose a single one of those vantage points.

Rather than run a risk of losing them we'll blow them to hell without waiting for the strategic moment. You understand?"

"Yes, sir."

"And lastly, I want prisoners from among the official ranks of the government forces. I want any high-ranking officer of the police, army, navy or intelligence service brought to me in sufficiently good condition to answer questions. We've got to get every possible scrap of information possible as to plans, movements of troops and ships, and exactly how serious they are in this threat of attacking the city. And I want to ask those questions *myself!* I'm not relying on anyone else at this time."

"Yes, sir."

"You may go."

The three officers left the room and Ellison was alone with Brace. The one-armed commander of the revolutionists stood so that he could see his own reflection in the full length mirror. He was a strange, very forceful figure at that moment. Even the cynical Brace recognized it as he exhaled a lungful of cigarette smoke toward the ceiling. Mad Ellison might be, but he had the courage of a lion and his tactical genius as a commander could not be questioned.

"You really mean to use gas?"

"Why not?" the general snarled. "We know how effective it is from the use we put it to at the Piney village. Government chemists haven't had time to prepare their men with equipment that will withstand it. If we are faced by a superior force we must use the weapons we have which will make us equal."

Brace's fingers shook a little as he raised his cigarette to his lips. "You know what that means," he said. "Every living, breathing creature in this city, not equipped with protective masks, will be dead in an hour. I saw what this stuff could do in the swamps."

The general's eyes flamed. "We are not here to consider weaklings who are not prepared to fight for the cause of right, Mr. Brace. There is no half-way measure for winning our fight. If the government forces us to brutalities then the responsibility is theirs, not ours! We have set out to gain control, and we are going to gain control!"

Let your beard grow for three days. Wear an old suit, wet it, let it dry on you; sleep in it. Do not wash your face and hands, or your eyes. Do not brush your hair. Rub iron rust into your hands and neck and face and let it seep in beneath your fingernails. At the end of three days your own mother won't know you.

DOMINICK VANE remembered these instructions on disguise which had been handed out to him when he first joined the Department of Justice. He was in the grimy little room of a mid-town hotel, about an hour after his visit to General Trent. He stood before the smudged mirror in the bathroom, looking at himself. There was no time for the elaborate preparations in disguise suggested by the department, but the face that stared back at Dominick from the glass gave him something of a shock. There had been no time to shave for the last two days and a dark stubble of beard covered his chin and cheeks. His usually sleek black hair, grayed slightly at the temples, was matted and unkempt looking. His eyes, sunk in their sockets, were red from lack of sleep and fatigue. There were deep scratches on one side of his face where Moxelli's sharp nails had dug at him. His clothes were rumpled and torn from that same struggle. As he looked at himself Dominick decided that he had come pretty close to acquiring that suggested disguise without doing much about it.

From the window of his room he could see one of the Red Sleeve recruiting stations in Times Square. It seemed to be doing a brisk business. Apparently a great many men had decided that the balance of power lay with the revolutionists, and they were hopping aboard before it was too late. Well, that was to be his job, too.

He had three days in which to get evidence that must be guarded so closely that even high officials in the Red Sleeve organization did not guess at its existence! Three days in which to find Dawson and make him talk! Three days to find Angela—

if she still lived! (It seemed like an eternity to him since that brief sweet moment when he had held her in his arms and kissed her!) Three days to find Philip Jaxon, who had thrown himself so recklessly into the fray—if he still lived!

For one bitter moment Dominick felt a flood of resentment sweep over him! What sin was he expiating that forever forced on him the loss of the people he loved, that prevented him from ever finding the peace and contentment that is a man's right. He had a right to Angela, and to happiness! And yet he must force her into the background of his mind. He must set his teeth and walk into the enemy circle, risking everything in an almost impossible quest. For what?

"... *during every waking moment I shall be praying for you,"* the President had written. *"You must be the instrument of God...."*

Now Dominick saw again those faces... thousands of twisted, agonized faces waiting in mortal dread for the scarlet Saturday to come! And behind them he saw the leering spectres of Dawson, Moxelli, Brace, men driven by greed to strike at the heart of their own country and its people! It was worth a thousand lives like his to bring about their defeat, Dominick thought.

Grimly he made a bundle of the things he would have to leave behind him. His letter from the President he burned. His Department of Justice credentials, his shoulder holster and the gun it contained, the tailor's labels from his suit. All these things must be discarded before he faced a recruiting officer.

OUT IN Times Square a curious crowd, dozens deep, made a circle around the old voting booth that had been turned into a recruiting station. Squatting on the pavement outside the building were a half-a-dozen Red Sleeves prepared to operate four machine guns that were set up, ready to take care of any loyalist demonstration in the mob.

Slowly Dominick edged his way through the crowd toward the clearing. People looked at him curiously as he started across the open space toward the building. In some faces he saw silent approval—in many he saw an unspoken anger. Before he reached the building one of the Red Sleeves blocked his way.

"Recruit?"

Dominick nodded, eyes downcast, cigarette between his lips, feet shuffling as though he were awkwardly nervous. Quickly the man ran his hands over Dominick's clothing in an expert "frisk."

"Okay," said the man. "Inside."

A recruiting officer sat at a desk. Two men, armed with rifles stood behind him. A civilian stood by the desk, answering questions. Dominick listened and prepared himself as best he could. The officer scarcely looked at him when it came his turn.

"Name?"

"Ray Brown," said Dominick coolly.

"Business?"

"Dock worker," said Dominick, cigarette bobbing between his lips.

"Address."

Dominick laughed, a short, staccato laugh. "Any one of a number of Park benches I could mention."

"Out of work, eh?" The man looked up, but there was no interest in his glance.

"Out of work and anxious to get a crack at some of the rats that have kept me there!" snapped Dominick.

"What can you do?"

"I was a sharpshooter during the World War," said Dominick. It was the first word of truth he had spoken.

"Handle a rifle, eh?"

"I could once," said Dominick.

The man scribbled something on a piece of paper. "Main entrance to Madison Square Garden," he said. "We're outfitting recruits there. If you can handle a gun we can use you."

"The fighting can't come too soon to suit me," said Dominick, "if there's a square meal thrown in somewhere!"

"They're handing out coffee and hot dogs up there," said the man. He nodded toward the other recruit, an Italian. "This guy's name is Ferrotti. You two trek along together."

Dominick looked at the Italian. "Okay, pal, let's go," he said.

The two men went out of the recruiting booth and started west toward Eighth Avenue. They walked in silence for a moment. Dominick stole a glance or two at his companion, sullen-faced, broad shouldered man, a pretty tough looking specimen.

"How come you joined up?" Dominick finally asked him.

Ferrotti shrugged. "Like you—outa work. Italy done all right under a dictator. I guess Uncle Sam could stand a good two-fisted guy in charge of things."

Dominick chuckled. "I guess you'd have to call Ellison a good one-fisted guy, wouldn't you?"

"Yeah, I guess so," said Ferrotti unsmiling.

They walked another block in silence. "What do you think about the President's proclamation?" Dominick asked.

"The government wouldn't have the nerve to open up on this town," said Ferrotti harshly. "They'd be cuttin' their own throats by killin' their own people. They won't dare."

"I'm not so sure," said Dominick. "They're in a spot."

"Well, suppose they do?" Ferrotti argued. "The Red Sleeves has got all the important places. I ain't so sure we couldn't lick 'em in a straightaway fight with a smart guy like Ellison bossin' the job."

"There are some other smart guys in the outfit, too," said Dominick. "Brace and Moxelli and that crowd." He hoped to draw something from the Italian, some gossip that might give him a notion of how the general public felt about things.

"Yeah, they're plenty smart, and tough too," said Ferrotti. "I guess I'm satisfied to string along with 'em. What the hell, we get shot if we don't. I'd rather have a gun in my hand when the shootin' starts."

"Me too," said Dominick.

THERE WERE huge crowds blocking Eighth Avenue and Forty-Ninth and Fiftieth Streets. As Dominick and Ferrotti worked their way through to the entrance of the Garden men shouted at them.

"There go a couple more suckers!"

Somebody smacked the man who had shouted. There were cheers. "America for Americans!" A Red Sleeve officer met them at the entrance and examined the slips of paper the recruiting officer had given them.

"Down that passage to the right," he said. "You have to see the main cheese before you can get outfitted."

Through the opening into the arena Dominick saw a long line of men being dealt out uniforms, guns, and other equipment. The business of recruiting was evidently going well. They started down the passage the guard had indicated. And suddenly Dominick felt his heart turn to ice. There was a gun jammed in his ribs. He spun around.

"Don't move or I'll blow the insides out of you!" snarled Ferrotti. He had a service revolver in his hand and his face was dark with purpose. "You dirty stool pigeon!"

"What are you talking about?" Dominick demanded steadily.

"You're coming with me to see the Chief," snapped the Italian. "You can do your talking then!"

"Have you gone crazy?" Dominick's voice was cool, even.

"Yeah! Crazy. I ain't no recruit, Mr. Ray Brown, see? It's my job to hear what you guys have to say and find out if you're okay. You know too much. Moxelli and Brace! There's been no publicity about them, wise guy. You wouldn't know about them unless you were on the inside. And if you was on the inside you wouldn't be enlisting at no recruiting station! Now march! Up them stairs!"

Laughter welled up in Dominick's throat and he had to fight desperately to keep it back. He had failed! And with such tragic swiftness that even the gods must be laughing. He had been guilty of the most cardinal sin that any intelligence officer can be guilty of. He had underrated an opponent. He had taken Ferrotti for granted, not stopping to realize that at this time the Red Sleeves would be doubly cautious about the men they recruited.

Very slowly he trudged up the stone stairs, Ferrotti's gun pressed hard in the small of his back. As they walked the Italian contented himself by calling Vane every foul name he could think of in English, Italian, Sicilian and some other dialects which Dominick couldn't recognize. Dominick wasn't afraid of Ferrotti. Ferrotti! Ferrotti was a little atom in the scheme of things, which made his success in trapping the government agent a bitter pill to swallow.

Dominick's mind was racing through a half-dozen possible stories he could tell the commanding officer which would account for his knowledge about Moxelli and Brace. He might be able to squeeze through this thing yet. He could say he had been a friend of Samuel Seaver, and that Seaver had told him about Brace and Moxelli. Seaver was dead and could not contradict his tale. He knew a lot about Seaver; where he had lived; what he looked like; tricks and mannerisms of speech. Seaver had been an agent of the Red Sleeves—albeit a pretty poor one. Still, Dominick felt that he might stand a chance of talking his way out of this spot.

THEY HAD come to the door of an office which had a few days before been the Garden superintendent's.

"Open her up!" ordered Ferrotti.

It was a small square office with cement floor and walls and one large window that was above the line of vision even of so tall a man as Dominick. There were pictures of fighters, hockey players, and bike riders on the wall. A man in a gray uniform sat at a desk, head bowed, writing. Behind him lounged a couple of guards.

"I got a stool pigeon here, Boss," said Ferrotti proudly.

"Oh yes?" the man at the desk looked up.

Every last ounce of courage, hope and strength Dominick had seemed to desert him in that moment. He felt the room whirling dizzily about his head. The commanding officer was Lefty Brace himself!

For a moment Brace stared at him blankly and then very slowly a one-sided smile twisted his lips and a cruel gleam came into his eyes.

"Well, well, well," he said, very softly.

Dominick fought back his nausea—nausea brought on by the grim realization that this was ultimate defeat. A strange, irrational thought pounded inside his head. In that moment he was not thinking of his country, or the mission in which he had failed, or even of Angela. He was thinking: "I must die with dignity. I mustn't give this man one moment of satisfaction."

Ferrotti was bubbling over with his story, unaware of the drama in the meeting of these two men. There would have been more pride in his voice had he known that his prisoner was the one man in all the government forces the Red Sleeves were most anxious to capture. Brace wasn't listening to the story. He had risen from his desk chair and stood looking at Dominick, moistening his lips.

"All right, Ferrotti, all right!" he said suddenly, harshly. "You've done well. Now get back to your post."

Reluctantly Ferrotti retired. Still Brace said nothing. Dominick looking into the cruel, shifty eyes, could almost read the man's thoughts. He felt a chill run along his spine. Then Brace snapped an order.

"Search him!"

The two guards went roughly over Dominick. There was nothing to find.

"Tie him to that post," ordered Brace, indicating a round steel pillar.

They shoved Dominick against the post, and handcuffs were snapped over his wrists from behind. A strap bit cruelly into the flesh of his legs. Apparently other prisoners had been fastened this way, for the men moved without hesitation.

"Now get out!" said Brace.

The guards looked at him in evident surprise.

"Get out!" Brace thundered. And then suddenly his voice sank to a cold, deadly quietness. "I want to be alone with this prisoner."

CHAPTER XVII

INQUISITION

VERY SLOWLY BRACE came around from behind his desk, his eyes never shifting from Dominick's face. He moved with a soft, noiseless tread, smiling, gently massaging the knuckles of his closed right fist with his left hand.

Dominick knew what was coming. His impulse was to tug futilely at the handcuffs that held his hands behind his back, but he knew that to struggle would only add to Brace's satisfaction in the situation. So he stood perfectly still, steeling himself to the ordeal that lay before him.

Now Brace was only a couple of feet away. Dominick could see the little bloodshot veins in the man's eyes… could feel his hot breath…. Brace was in no hurry. He just stood there, looking at his prisoner and rubbing his knuckles.

"I hadn't hoped for this moment to come so soon, Vane," he said, voice soft, purring. "The first time we met you called me a heel; the second time, you hit me when my guard was down. It seems to me it's my turn now."

Dominick stood there, tight-lipped, silent.

"You can dish it out, all right, Vane. You gave Moxelli quite a beating up. But it may interest you to know that he suffered no permanent ill effects—except that he's quite sore at you, Vane. You see, his girl got killed in the mix-up. Most unfortunate for you if Mox gets his hands on you."

A man can take only so much, Dominick was thinking. After a while he becomes unconscious or dies. It couldn't last very much longer and all he had to do was to take it without giving Brace any satisfaction.

"Aren't you going to speak a little piece for me, Vane?" Brace asked sardonically. "I expected you would lash me with rhetoric—call me naughty names. You disappoint me, Vane. Don't all heroes make speeches about God and country and the purity of American womanhood before they get the works? Ah, well—I suppose I can't have everything."

And then he struck. A slashing right uppercut to Dominick's unprotected jaw that drove his head snapping back against the steel post. The double impact sent his knees sagging. Bright spots of pain danced before his eyes. But he stood upright.

Something like murder was in Brace's eyes. He swung again, right and left, to the mouth, to the point of the chin. He seemed to work himself into a frenzy. He kicked savagely at Dominick's shins, his powerful fists tore at Dominick's stomach. It was as if all the pent-up hatred of a lifetime were being taken out in this brutal assault.

"Keep standing! Keep on your feet." Dominick kept saying that to himself. There was a red fog before his face through which he could only see his attacker vaguely. His knees kept sagging, and he kept pulling himself up, trying to keep his chin sunk in on his chest so those terrible blows to the head did not send him slamming back against the steel upright.

Brace was unrelenting in the fury of his attack. At last human flesh could stand no more and very slowly Dominick sank down the post to the floor. The toe of Brace's heavy, military boot caught him back of the ear as he fell and he remembered no more.

BRACE STOOD over him, sweat pouring off his face, breathing heavily from his fierce exertion. After a moment he delivered another kick at his unconscious prisoner and then he turned away. He looked as if he were disappointed because it had all been brief. He went to the office door and opened it.

"All right," he snapped at the men who waited outside.

They came back into the room, looking curiously at the fallen man.

"Get anything out of him, sir?" one of them asked.

"I'm taking him to Ellison," Brace said shortly. "He waits to ask the questions himself. This guy is a big shot—chief of the government Intelligence. Otherwise I'd have killed him." He stood behind his desk, straightening his black uniform-tie. "Unhitch him from that post but keep his hands locked behind him. Load him into my car and have a couple of men ready to take the trip with me. Ellison's gone to the country for a conference with the big shots. I'm taking him there."

How long he was unconscious Dominick didn't know. When he came to he was lying in a cramped position on the floor of a car which seemed to be moving at a considerable rate of speed. Tentatively he tried to move and every muscle in his body cried out in protest. He was in the back seat of the car and two men were sitting with their feet on him.

He lay perfectly still. He wanted a chance to do a little thinking without being roughed up again. His lips were thick, swollen, cut. A sharp pain in his side warned him that he had a broken or badly bruised rib. Then he heard Brace's voice from the front seat.

"Left turn up ahead here."

Brace and the driver up front; two men behind. It was ridiculous even to consider the possibility of escape with his hands manacled behind his back. He guessed he was being taken somewhere for questioning—probably to Ellison himself. It was ironic that in this instance there was very little he could tell the Red Sleeve commander even if he would. He knew the government planned to fight back—but Ellison knew that himself. There was nothing of importance they could force him to tell because he knew nothing.

To steel himself against the coming of death was all he could do. He had no illusions as to what the final outcome of this affair was to be. Brace, Moxelli and Dawson would demand his life. And Ellison would grant their request. After all, he was a spy.

Yet, even as he resigned himself to the inevitable, his senses were alert. His mind told him he was at the end of the road, but his spirit would not give up. He could not guess how long they had been traveling before he regained consciousness. They were taking him somewhere out of the city—that was certain. In the country there would be fewer guards. If they once freed his hands—left him alone for any time at all—there might be a chance.

Suddenly the wheels of the car crunched on gravel as they made a sharp turn. A moment later the car came to a halt.

"Drag him out!" was Brace's sharp order.

Rough hands seized him by the arms and pulled him out of the car. He managed to get his feet under him and stand. They were in front of a large Colonial house with sweeping lawns and beautifully kept gardens and shrubbery. Red Sleeve guards stood on the little terrace that led to the front door.

"So you came to," drawled Brace, looking at the battered government agent.

DOMINICK WAS swaying on his feet, his head light, aching. The Red Sleeves took him by the arm and dragged him across the driveway and up the path to the house. Brace gave crisp orders and they were admitted to the house.

"Keep him here," said Brace, "while I have a chat with the general."

The guards let Dominick sit down on a bench at the foot of a beautiful spiral staircase that led to the floor above. The guards apparently had no intention of baiting their prisoner. One of them was almost solicitous.

"Want a drag on this, buddy?" he asked, holding the cigarette he had been smoking to Dominick's lips.

"Thanks." Dominick drew the smoke hungrily into his lungs. He looked up at the guard. "Where are we? Whose place is this?"

"Sorry. We can't do any talking," said the man. He smiled dryly. "I guess you'll be taking the same line yourself."

"I guess so," Dominick admitted.

"You're just out of luck, bein' on the wrong side of the fence with these guys," said the guard. "They don't play nice. But I guess you found that out already."

Then suddenly the guard snatched the cigarette from Dominick's lips and crushed it out under his heel. He stood at attention as Brace came along the hall.

"Can you walk?" Brace rapped at Dominick, "Or do we have to carry you into the General's office?"

"Oh, I can walk," said Dominick quietly.

"This way, then."

Unsteadily Dominick preceded Brace along the hall to the room at its end. As he stepped across the threshold his muscles tightened. This was the works and no mistake. He had never seen Ellison in the flesh, but he recognized him immediately. The general sat at a big desk, staring out from beneath his shaggy eyebrows. Beside him was H.R. Dawson, suave, smiling smugly as the prisoner's eyes met his. Behind the banker, a large patch of adhesive tape on the side of his head, was Moxelli, thick lips twisted, eyes fixed hungrily on Dominick as if he couldn't wait his chance. Corbet and Frampton were there too. This was the high council of the Red Sleeves—the real powers of the Revolution. And Dominick faced them, helpless, hands locked behind him. These were the men he had been hunting, but he had found them too late.

Ellison was the first to speak: "You are Dominick Vane?"

"Yes."

"You are accused of attempting espionage in our ranks. Is that true?"

"Would it make any difference if I denied it?" Dominick asked dryly.

"You know the war-time penalty for spies?"

"Yes."

"Have you any interest in living, Mr. Vane?"

Dominick's eyes were hard as he met the general's stare steadily. "Are you proposing a bargain, General?"

"What are the government's plans?" Ellison rapped.

"You know them as well as I do, General."

"Do you really think they mean to go through with it or are they bluffing?"

Dominick's bruised lips moved in a faint smile. "What do you think?" he countered.

Dawson leaned forward, fingering the tip of his waxed gray mustache with slender fingers. There was a mocking note in his voice. "You know, Mr. Vane, you have been a great nuisance to us from the start. You stumble over our plans before we are ready and force us to act ahead of schedule. You force some of us into hiding. You beat up our men. You have influenced my family against me. Really, Mr. Vane, you have put us to no end of trouble."

"The pleasure," said Dominick dryly, "is all mine."

"But that pleasure has come to an end, Mr. Vane," Dawson said softly. "Now it's our turn for a little fun. There are several of us who would like to have a minute or two with you alone."

"Especially," said Dominick, his cold eyes shifting to Brace, "if my hands are tied behind me."

"Tut, tut, let us have no recriminations," Dawson drawled. "You must see, Mr. Vane, that whatever your prowess as a fighter may be, we hold all the cards now. I admire bravery. As a matter of fact, I must confess to a sneaking admiration for your own qualities along that line. But I would like you to see that bravery isn't going to do you any good."

"So what?" said Vane.

DAWSON SIGHED like a man who is having difficulty with a recalcitrant child. "Mr. Vane, you are chief of the President's flying squadron of intelligence men. You know the government plans. You know what military maneuvers they intend making. In short you are just brimming with information of an accurate nature. We don't want to force you to talk. In fact we are willing to bargain with you as you suggested. Give us the information we want and we will overlook the little matter of the firing squad."

Dominick eyed the banker steadily. "Mr. Dawson, your lack of intelligence is a constant source of amazement to me. You have made some rather serious mistakes since the beginning of this affair. And you are making another one now."

"Don't waste time with him," Moxelli snarled. "We'll make him talk!"

"We have found one very effective method," Dawson went on, his eyes fixed thoughtfully on the ceiling. "The driving of fine wire nails up under the fingernails seems to be most effective. It's a method that seems to break down the strongest of men. Some of them scream, Vane. It is a very distressing sound. They scream, and, at last, they talk."

The jaw muscles under Dominick's cheeks rippled. "I have no special information to give you if I would," he said. "Of course you won't believe that."

"Of course," said Dawson. He looked at Ellison. The beetle-browed general made a sudden sharp gesture with his thumb.

Instantly Dominick was seized from behind. Strong hards fastened on his wrists and his hands were pressed flat on a table top. Dawson rose from his desk and sauntered over to a window, his back to Dominick. And then pain came, so agonizing that for all his will power a groan escaped Dominick's lips. There was the faint tapping sound of a hammer on a fine wire nail.

Then Dominick fainted. Dawson turned back from the window. His face was pale but perfectly composed, as he looked at the crumpled figure on the floor.

"Less resistance than I expected," he said. "He must be pretty well all-in. Perhaps later...."

"Put him down stairs," snapped Ellison.

Consciousness of a sort returned swiftly to Dominick. He was aware that he was being carried out of the room, and then down a steep flight of stairs. Suddenly they dropped him, and his body bounced down over three or four steps to a concrete floor. He lay still, too weak to move, too racked with pain. He could hear the footsteps of the men who had carried him retreating up the stairs and the slamming of a door.

The cement was cool against his hot face. And then, suddenly, very gentle hands were lifting him to a more comfortable position.

"Take it easy, old man." It was a familiar voice, but Dominick didn't place it for the moment.

Then there was a startled cry: "Philip! It's Dominick!"

Dominick opened his eyes, incredulous. The light was very dim but he could see Angela's face. Then her cheek was against his….

"Oh, my darling, my darling!"

Dominick tried to speak but nothing happened. And then he faded again, very gently this time, into unconsciousness.

CHAPTER XVIII

THREE ABOUT TO DIE

IT WAS PART of the cellar, but it had been made over into a sort of game room—this place where the prisoners were held. There was a ping-pong table, a couple of card tables. Around the walls benches had been built and they were covered with upholstered cushions. One of these Philip Jaxon stretched on the floor.

Very gently he lifted Dominick Vane's bruised body on it.

"The devils!" he said between his teeth. "They've been torturing him, Angela!"

Angela sat at one end of the cushion with Dominick's head in her lap. "Get me some water, Philip," she said, in a level voice.

A moment later she was bathing Dominick's face, washing the dirt and blood from his torn lips. "Take your handkerchief and work it under those handcuffs so that they won't cut into his flesh," she directed Philip. "Oh please be careful of his finger. They've—they've driven a nail into his thumb!"

"I'll get it out while he's still unconscious," said Philip grimly. "You won't want to see this."

Angela turned her face away. Philip swore softly under his breath. A shudder of agony shook Dominick's body and he opened his eyes. He saw Angela. So it hadn't been a dream of delirium. She was here.

"It's really you, Angela?" he whispered.

"It's really me, darling," she said. "Philip is here, too."

"Damn Philip," he said, and tried to grin. He turned his head to look up into Philip's white face. "You all right, fella?"

143

"The hell with me. Of course I'm all right," said Philip. "But what have they done to you, Dominick? Why have they brought you here?"

"I got caught," said Dominick simply. He looked back at Angela. He wanted to take her in his arms, but they were fastened tight behind him. He felt a sudden choking lump in his throat. He was never going to hold her in his arms again. There could be little doubt of that. "You, Angela—you're all right!"

"Yes, yes, Dominick. They brought me here shortly after I phoned you in Washington. You knew that I'd phoned you?"

"I knew, Angela," he said. "I tried to come at once; I couldn't."

"Oh Dominick, don't be silly. I knew you couldn't. Things

had started happening when I called you. After that the phone service went off. But what *is* going on? Philip and I know nothing. They've kept us here for several days."

Briefly Dominick told them the situation in New York and the country at large. He told them how he'd been caught. "I had to take chances, with only three days to work in," he said in conclusion.

"What will they do to you now?" Angela asked tensely.

Dominick tried to smile. "Let's not talk about that, darling. Let's talk about the things that might have been. We may not have long. They'll be coming back for me when they think I can talk a little more." His voice hardened.

"Dominick!" Angela was sobbing. He felt the warm splash of a tear against his cheek.

"Hey, this will never do," he said gently. "I played a long shot and lost. I'll have to pay. But you and Philip are going to be all right. Dawson will see to that."

"I wonder," said Philip Jaxon in a tight voice. "There are a lot of things to tell you, Dominick. Angela and I know too much for comfort."

Dominick turned his head. "What do you mean?" he asked sharply.

"It was Angela who found it out," said Philip. "Perhaps she'd better tell you."

Dominick looked at her and his heart suddenly pounded against his ribs. If these two had put themselves on the spot on his account...!

ANGELA BEGAN to talk, her fingers cool on his forehead. As Dominick listened he could scarcely believe his ears: "It happened after you left for Washington, Dominick. You'd told me what you suspected about my uncle, and while I believed that you believed what you said... well, just for a little, I thought you must be wrong. You see, he'd always been so decent to me. Somehow... somehow I couldn't take it in. Then he acted so peculiarly to you about Philip. I knew something was wrong.

Still I thought perhaps uncle wasn't really responsible. It wasn't lack of faith in you, Dominick. It was...."

"I know, darling. Go on," he urged her.

"Well, I did a little snooping. Uncle was out of his study. I began going through things and—and, in a nutshell, Dominick, it's this. There are written contracts—proof of this whole scheme. Ellison is to be dictator; uncle and his friends are to control all the natural resources: mines, oil, wells, gold. They make Ellison dictator by financing the revolution. He pays them back by giving them all the government concessions!"

"You mean to tell me they have *written* contracts that state those facts?" Dominick cried. "Do you realize what it would mean if they could be publicized? If we could prove that grasping capitalists are really back of this whole thing?"

"Oh Dominick, its my fault that it isn't possible!" Angela said. "But I was afraid. I should have taken them—run out of the house—hidden until I could get them to you. But they were shooting in the streets. I lost my nerve. So I left them where they were and phoned you in Washington. I found Moxelli's address too. But I didn't have the courage." This with a tragic bitterness.

"I wouldn't have wanted you to risk it," said Dominick. "But written contracts—!" He sounded dazed.

"Every one of 'em has a copy of it," said Philip Jaxon. "—Sort of insurance. But what I was driving at, is that they know we know it. I—well—I blew off my fool mouth to my uncle. After that they stuck us down here and I don't know what they mean to do with us. But one thing is certain. They aren't going to let us go free to tell what we know."

"So you see, Dominick," Angela said, "we're in something of a spot ourselves." She said it almost proudly, as if she were glad to be sharing his danger with him.

Dominick closed his eyes. If anyone could get a copy of that contract—! But who would ever know about it. He knew that he was not going to manage it, and he knew that Philip was right when he said Dawson would never let them go. How could word be gotten to anyone on the outside? They wouldn't dare attempt bribing one of the guards! But—there must be some way!

Yet as the hours ticked away the government agent was forced to admit that they were up against a blank wall. Escape was out; getting a message through was out; and Dominick, with his hands manacled behind his back, couldn't even count himself in the picture. Whatever they intended to do with him would not include a chance of playing any further part in the scheme of things.

Hot, feverish, exhausted, he lay on that cushion, his head in Angela's lap, struggling for a vision of some solution, until at last he slept. For days he had been going at top speed and now he could hold out no longer against the crying need for rest.

WHEN HE opened his eyes it seemed to him that he could not have slept long; yet there was a pillow under his head now. He twisted around and saw that Angela was stretched out on one of the benches, also sleeping. Philip was hunched over in a chair, cigarette between his lips, eyes red-rimmed. As Dominick moved Philip spoke:

"Feeling better?"

Dominick tried moving his legs gingerly. He grinned. "I guess so. How long have I been sleeping?"

Philip laughed. "Seventeen hours and eleven minutes according to my watch. You must have been all in."

"Seventeen hours!" Dominick sat bolt upright! "You're kidding!"

"Not at all," said Philip. "You didn't come to, even when our charming friends from upstairs brought food. Angela thought it was best not to disturb you."

Seventeen hours! It had been late afternoon of Wednesday when he went to sleep. Now it was early afternoon Thursday— the second of the three precious days allotted him to do his job. With everything depending on him, he had slept around the clock. And yet, he bitterly reflected, there was nothing he could have done had he been awake.

Philip had saved some food for him and he fed him—since Dominick could not use his own hands. Then one of Philip's cigarettes, and Dominick began to feel really better. He and Philip talked softly so as not to disturb Angela. Philip had no idea whose house this was; but he did know that it was somewhere in the neighborhood of White Plains.

"And we have to sit here and twiddle our thumbs with the bloodiest slaughter in history coming up—unless we can spill the beans!" Philip groaned.

Dominick smiled dryly. "I might point out, my friend, that I can't even do any thumb twiddling with these irons on!"

Angela woke a little later. Together they talked in and out and around their problem. She could add nothing to the fast dwindling stock of Dominick's hopes.

"I suppose we might as well face the fact that they'll probably shoot the lot of us for spies," Philip said. "It sickens me when I think of the years I have liked my uncle—even admired him!"

"The lust for power is a terrible thing when it gets in a man's blood, Philip," Dominick said gravely. "Ellison is a fine soldier and he once was a man of very high character. But the chance for power has made a lunatic of him! And he and your uncle have come so far now they can never turn back!"

And, then, suddenly, men were coming down stairs again. Four of the Red Sleeves confronted them.

"You're wanted upstairs again," the leader rapped.

Painfully stiff, Dominick needed Philip's aid to stand. He turned to Angela. "I guess it's goodbye, darling," he said very gently. "Do you mind if I say it once?"

"Say it, Dominick?"

"—That I love you!"

"Oh, my darling." She was suddenly very close to him, clinging to him.

"Make it snappy," the guard officer said harshly. "You're all going up this time."

"All?"

"That's what I said!"

DOMINICK HAD always been a fatalist about himself. He had taken on a dangerous job, and death, he knew, was never far from him. He was ready for it. But Angela and Philip! They had a right to life. If he had not taken Philip as a guide that day in the swamps of Marshfield neither of them would be in this spot; and having got them in it he was utterly powerless to do anything about getting them out of it!

He managed to speak softly to Angela as they reached the top of the stair. "Keep your nerve, darling," he said. "They may try to frighten you with threats. But I'm certain Dawson won't let any harm come to you." As he said it Dominick wished fervently that he believed it. Dawson—all of them—were drunk with a dream of untold wealth and power. There was precious little they wouldn't do to reach their goal.

Angela's fingers pressed Dominick's arm gently. "We'll see it through somehow," she said.

They were taken back to the room at the end of the corridor. Ellison still sat at the big flat-topped desk, chin sunk in the palm of his hand, his eyes blazing darkly as he surveyed the prisoners. Dawson was over at one of the windows, his back turned. He didn't look around as they came in. Moxelli and Brace sat on either side of the general. There was a long silence as the three prisoners stood side by side, facing this tribunal. At last the general spoke in a harsh impatient voice:

"Mr. Vane, we have neither the time nor the inclination to battle with your stubborn refusal to talk. I have had you brought here to give you one last chance, of your own volition, to tell me what I want to know. I offered to trade you your life for that information. You refused. That offer is no longer open to you."

"I never counted very heavily on your keeping your part of the bargain," said Dominick coolly.

"I am not much of a hand at repartee, Mr. Vane," said Ellison sourly. "I will be as brief as possible. These two other prisoners, Miss Dawson and Mr. Jaxon, are admittedly in possession of information we cannot afford to have broadcast. It is not my fault that they chose to involve themselves in this affair. As you know, Mr. Dawson tried every way he knew to keep Jaxon, here, out of it. As a matter of fact he jeopardized our whole cause by trying to get him out of the mess which you, Mr. Vane, dragged him into. But these two young people have insisted on meddling. And so they have become so dangerous to us that we have no choice left. They must be dealt with as any other spy would be."

Dominick moistened his lips. "You mean…?"

"Firing squad!" the general rapped. His gaze never left Dominick's face. He saw the deadly pallor that swept over it—saw the fear. "You have been a soldier, Mr. Vane. You must see that we have no other choice!"

Dominick drew a deep breath. "Yes, I have been a soldier, general," he said slowly. "I fought to 'make the world safe for democracy.' I have even admired you as a soldier and a man. But I would not have believed you could sink so low as to become an executioner of innocent people to satisfy your own selfish ends!"

"Selfish!" Ellison's voice cracked like a pistol shot. "Do you call it selfish to be ridding the country of the blood-sucking politicians and capitalist slave-drivers that have been feeding off it for years?"

"So you can put other capitalists in power?" Dominick asked grimly. "I know you had to have money to finance your cause! But you've hogtied yourself by getting help from the same kind of men you're fighting!"

ELLISON MADE an impatient gesture. "I am not here to argue ethics with you, Mr. Vane. I am here to pass sentence on you three prisoners. And that sentence is death!"

"Just a moment, General," said Dominick passionately. "I'm not pleading for myself. I ran a risk and lost. I'm ready to die. But these others are different. You're overestimating the danger they can be to you. They know that certain contracts exist between you and your backers. But the facts contained in those contracts are already known to me, to the powers that be in Washington.

I'll be frank with you. My job was to find proof of these facts. Well, I've failed."

"And *how!*" said Lefty Brace unpleasantly.

Dominick ignored him. "But if you let these youngsters go, even if they shouted what they know from the housetops it wouldn't be dangerous to you. It will be shouted by someone else whatever happens."

"They saw the proof with their own eyes!" said Ellison grimly. "Their word would carry weight. They are relatives of Mr. Dawson's."

"But you *can't* do this," Dominick said despairingly.

"Don't plead for us," Philip said angrily. "Sure. We're related to H.R. Dawson. But I don't want anything from him and I don't think Angela does. There'll be plenty of lives lost putting him and his double-crossing, chiseling friends where they belong. I'll be proud if my life is one of them."

Lefty Brace smiled a thin, twisted smile. "Listen!—it's one of the Rover boys in the flesh," he said sardonically.

An infinite sense of futility swept over Dominick as he looked into Ellison's unrelenting eyes. "Let me say one more thing—" he began. "These two youngsters are not guilty of espionage. They stumbled over certain facts by accident. Imprison them if you think they are dangerous, but if there is any mercy in your heart at all, let them live."

Ellison's face was like a granite mask. "Mr. Vane, I am fighting for a cause—a cause I believe in with all my heart and soul. Unfortunately, for the ultimate good, it has been necessary for me to make deals which might be misunderstood. These young people know about those deals. In a few days I shall be dictator of this country! If that first victory were all, I would let them go. I am not a butcher at heart, Mr. Vane. But the information these two have is not only dangerous to me and to my cause now—it would also be equally dangerous *at any time in the future!* Do you understand that?"

Very slowly Dominick nodded. He understood. There was

something compelling about this one-armed madman. He believed in himself and his destiny with an almost religious fervor.

"I cannot allow anything to interfere with my purpose, Mr. Vane," Ellison concluded.

There was a moment of dead silence. Then Angela spoke in a very steady voice:

"May God have mercy on your soul, General Ellison."

And through all this Dawson had not once turned from the window or spoken.

CHAPTER XIX

A WESTCHESTER GARDEN

"MACLYN!" ELLISON SNAPPED. "You will take these prisoners into the garden, arm a firing squad, and dispose of them."

A white-faced officer stepped forward from the door where he had been standing. He saluted. "Very good, sir!"

The other guards stepped forward—two for each of them. Something seemed to go dead in Dominick as they took him by the arms and turned him around. A firing squad in a Westchester garden…! He couldn't quite believe in the reality of the scene. Four or five days ago none of them had dreamed that life didn't stretch out sweetly ahead of them. Angela, young, beautiful, happy at living; Jaxon, with his polo ponies, his dogs, his beautiful country estate; Dominick himself, holding down a dangerous job, but with that incurable optimism of all humans concerning death.

Now death was a matter of minutes.

They were being marched along the corridor to the front door. They were out into the open. There was the fragrance of the flowers in the garden that was presently to be wet with their blood. Oh—it was mad! It was one of those dreams that had plagued Dominick for years…. Yet strong fingers gripped his arms—their pressure painfully real. And Angela and Philip were walking ahead of him. He could see the imprint of their feet on the soft earth of the garden path. It was real enough! God pity them—it was real.

In the center of the garden was a little rock pool. Lilies floated on its surface and there was a stone figure—a dancing satyr, water spurting from the trumpet it blew. A chipmunk ran past busily, not six inches from Dominick's feet. It was late afternoon. Somewhere a bird sang lustily, with the joy of living!

This couldn't happen!

Yet they were being led toward a high, boxwood hedge. Behind him he heard the rattle of rifles as a squad of gray-shirted men assembled at a curt order from Maclyn. Then they were being turned around against the boxwood to face their fate: twelve grim-faced men with rifles.

Dominick could see Angela and Philip now. Angela was very calm. They stood close enough to one another so that she was able to reach out and touch his hand.

"Don't worry, darling," she said. "Perhaps—perhaps there is something after this…."

Dominick couldn't answer. His lips were stiff with horror and they refused to move. Philip, very white, stood rigidly. His legs spread a little apart, as if to withstand the jarring shock that was to come.

Maclyn stood in front of them for a moment. He was look-ing at Angela. "I would give my right arm not to have to do this, Miss Dawson," he said.

"It's your job," said Angela.

Maclyn turned and walked back toward the waiting men. Dominick took a deep, hungry breath. He wanted all of the sweet air he could draw into his lungs. He wanted to hold Ange-la's hand, but the manacles prevented it.

And then something made Dominick's heart stop beating entirely for an instant. A voice spoke to him from behind the hedge.

"When the fun begins, folks, run, do not walk, to the near-est exit!"

Johnny Harbold! Dominick whispered his name, unbelieving, dizzy with hope.

"IN PERSON, not a moving picture," said Johnny Harbold softly. "Please do not show surprise, ladies and gentlemen. You are about to witness a very unusual spectacle. News, in fact. Man bites dog—firing squad shot as it is about to fire! Too bad you haven't any cotton to put in your ears because I'm going to make a hell of a lot of noise. *And run to the left*—because at this precise moment I am about to open fire with a machine gun on your right!"

Maclyn had almost reached his waiting squad. In a moment he would give his orders. Dominick was shaking. "Johnny...!"

"You told me to join the revolution, didn't you, Boss?" Johnny's voice asked lightly. "—Well, I always obey orders. Only I just had to kill a guy to get this machine gun. Won't the dear General be surprised?" And then his voice was suddenly sharp: *"Now!* Run like blazes!"

At the same instant, not a foot to the right of Dominick, the machine gun barked its staccato rattle of fire. The prisoners were running, running like mad. In one quick glance Dominick saw the firing squad go down like ninepins! Johnny kept firing. Men appeared on the terrace, and the machine gun raked them off....

Dominick was unable to make much headway with his arms locked behind him. Once he stumbled and fell heavily, grinding his face in the gravel path. Philip helped him up and they plunged on. And behind them Johnny Harbold's machine gun still snapped savagely.

They were following a sort of path; and then, ahead of them, loomed two things. A garage with several cars parked in front of it, and a man in a Red Sleeve uniform running toward them, evidently attracted by the fire. He was pulling a revolver from a holster at his side. Dominick could not use his hands but he was almost on top of the startled revolutionist and he threw a football block into him that would have brought joy to the heart of a big-time coach. Down went the man—and down came Philip on top of them both. Philip had the gun now. He pulled the trigger as the Red Sleeve tried to rise.

Angela had kept on running. She was already behind the wheel of a big touring car. Dominick stumbled drunkenly into the seat behind her. Still they could hear Johnny's machine gun spitting death. Philip delayed a moment—Philip, who was unused to this kind of thing, was keeping a very cool head on his shoulders. There were three other cars there. Up went their hoods. Viciously Philip ripped out wiring that would keep them out of service for hours. Angela had the touring car moving when he tumbled into the back seat with Dominick.

"These cuffs!" Dominick groaned.

"You'll have to roll down on the floor," said Philip. "There may be tools or something under this seat."

Dominick got on the floor. Meanwhile Angela was driving the car at breakneck speed down the drive, out through stone gates.

"Keep her down to the floor, kid," Philip shouted at her. "If anyone tries to stop you, ride over 'em."

He had got the back seat up. He found a screwdriver and a hammer.

"This is going to hurt," he told Dominick.

And as they were tossed around on the floor of the wildly-swaying car Philip began pounding at the lock on one of the cuffs. Dominick's lower lip was caught between his teeth. Each blow of the hammer on the screwdriver sent the other side of the cuff biting into his flesh brutally. Sweat poured off his face but he lay as still as he could, bracing himself with his feet. And then a cry of triumph rose from Philip.

"Got it!"

Dominick managed to pull himself back on the seat. The handcuffs still dangled from his right wrist. But his hands were free. Philip had an arm around his shoulder.

"You're all right, Dominick?"

Dominick wiped the sweat from his face with the back of a trembling hand.

"All right," he said.

HOW THAT girl could drive! And there was no sign of pursuit. It looked like a clean getaway.

"Who in heaven's name was that bird with the machine gun?" Philip asked.

"One of my men," said Dominick. "How he got there I don't know."

"I got a glimpse of him," said Philip. "He was in a Red Sleeve uniform."

Angela was slowing down. She spoke without looking back at them. "We seem to be coming into White Plains," she said. "Where do we go from here, Dominick?"

With an effort Dominick brought his mind back to the immediate problem. The closer they got to the city the greater the danger there would be of encountering Red Sleeves. There would be an alarm out for them. It would be better to head north until they could find a place to hide for a few hours and map out their plan of campaign.

And even as he was thinking this they swung around a bend in the road and an exclamation of alarm escaped Philip. Angela was jamming on the brakes. Philip had drawn the gun he had taken from the Red Sleeve guard. Ahead of them the road was jammed with men, motorcycles and cars.

"We can never drive through that mob!" Philip cried.

But Dominick Vane was laughing. "You idiots! Don't you see? They're government troops! Slow down, Angela, darling! We're going to let someone else think for us for a bit!"

As the car came to a halt they were quickly surrounded by soldiers. A young lieutenant came up briskly. He started to speak. Then he took one look at the battered and bloody Dominick and what he had to say was stilled on his lips. Dominick rose and got out of the car.

"I'm Dominick Vane," he said. "Chief of the President's Flying Squad. Unfortunately I have no credentials with me to prove it—unless you would consider my present condition an evidence of good faith!"

The lieutenant saluted smartly. "As a matter of fact, Mr. Vane, I've been on the lookout for you. I'm Lieutenant Greer, attached to General Trent's army. One of your men—chap named Harbold—got through a report that you'd been taken prisoner. Seems he'd managed to get on the inside himself, and—"

Dominick interrupted. "Harbold has just saved our lives, Lieutenant. We were on the point of being put to death by a firing squad when— But more of that later. Point is, Ellison, Dawson, Moxelli, Brace—the whole crew of them—are at a house about fifteen miles back along this road. If you and your men move fast we may be able to catch the lot of them."

"Can you lead the way?" Greer asked.

"Certainly."

"Then let's go." He placed a whistle to his lips and blew a shrill blast. Angela was already turning the car. Motorcycles and trucks roared into life. Greer got into the touring car with Dominick and the other two.

"I have about a hundred men here, six machine guns, grenades— We can do a pretty good job on 'em, I imagine. Anyhow we can try!"

It was almost dusk when they started spinning back along the highway. Suddenly, off to the left, a great flickering red light shot up into the sky. There were clouds of black smoke. Dominick gripped the lieutenant's arm.

"The house lies almost exactly in that direction. I hope we aren't going to be too late!"

AS THE cars and motorcycles raced through the growing dusk toward the leaping flames on the horizon any doubt that it was the Red Sleeve Headquarters which was burning was quickly dissolved. It was the big Westchester estate beyond question, and as they drew closer the wind blew whiffs of the dark, whirling smoke in their direction—a smoke pungent with the smell of oil.

"They must have been ready to touch it off at a moment's notice," Dominick said to the lieutenant.

"Why?" Greer asked.

Dominick shrugged. "They had to move in a hurry once we'd given them the slip. They probably knew we stood a good chance of running into detachments of government troops. No chance to transport records or other incriminating evidence that might have been there."

"You think they'll have gotten away themselves?"

"I think so, Lieutenant. We put three cars out of commission, but there were a couple of others at the front of the house." Dominick's lips were tight set. "If we could have nailed that whole bunch together, Greer, we'd have come mighty close to ending this thing right here and now. Without Ellison to command, and Dawson and the others to provide financial support, this little tea party would go up in smoke as quickly as that house is burning!"

Angela swung the touring car through the gates and brought it to a halt. Even at a distance of a hundred yards the intense heat reached them. Flames and smoke spurted from windows, upstairs and down.

The heat was blistering.

Greer ordered his men to spread a cordon around the place on the chance that there might still be Red Sleeves on the grounds. After that there was nothing to do but wait for the fire to subside sufficiently for them to approach closer.

Angela climbed out from behind the wheel and got into the back seat of the car with Dominick. She slipped her arm through his, but neither of them spoke. Somehow there was no need for talk.

It was nearly a half hour before the roof of the great house thundered into the foundations, sending a shower of burning wood up into the night air. And it was only then that Angela spoke.

"Do you think he got away, Dominick?"

"It's a pretty forlorn hope," said Dominick gravely.

They were both thinking of Johnny Harbold.

And later, when they were able to get close to the smoul-
dering ruins, they found him. Dominick went straight to that
boxwood hedge in front of which they had stood a little while
before waiting for the sentence of death to be carried out. The
front of the hedge had been scorched black by the fire, but
Johnny's body lay behind it. He was dead—struck by only one
bullet which had gone squarely through his heart. He had fallen
across the machine gun which he had stood by till he was hit.
He was smiling.

DOMINICK PICKED up the body and walked back to the car
with it. As he placed the body in the back seat that fury that he
had known once before in his life came to him. "I'll be collecting
for this in person, Johnny," he said. "I won't forget you, Johnny."

"Will they have destroyed those contracts in the fire?" Philip
asked.

There was in Dominick's eyes that diamond-hard light that
both Angela and Philip had seen there that first day in Marshfield. Angela, looking at him, realized that here, once more, was
the man-hunter, not the gentle, almost tender lover of their brief
moments of intimacy.

"Contracts or no contracts," he said, "I'm going to get the lot
of them. Now understand this, both of you. You saw those docu-
ments. You can both swear that they did exist! If you both rack
your brains you may even be able to recall phrases from them.
Keep thinking! Try to remember! Because, if they are destroyed,
when it comes to a showdown your testimony is going to be
important!"

"What do we do now, Dominick?" Angela asked quietly.

"We're going back to New York," said Dominick. "I'm going
to put you both somewhere you'll be safe. And you're going to
stay there and sit tight. Remember this. You haven't the right
to run risks. Your presence at the right time, alive and able to
give testimony, may be of the utmost importance." And then he
seemed to realize the severity of his manner, and for just a second
he relaxed. He dropped one hand on Philip's shoulder; the other

he slipped through Angela's arm. "It sounds like a pretty lurid speech, I know, but these are lurid times and the future of a great nation may depend on your being on deck at the right time. I'm aiming this especially at you, Philip. You've got to stay out of things until the time comes for you to do your part. We've got just a little more than thirty hours left. We've got to catch up with these guys by then. If we don't,"—his lips tightened—"it won't matter much what we do!"

"Philip and I will do exactly as you tell us, Dominick," Angela said.

"Good girl!" He was crisp, impersonal again. "And here's Greer."

The lieutenant came up and saluted. "They seem to have got away clean—the lot of them, Mr. Vane."

"I expected it," said Dominick. "Lieutenant, I've got to get back to New York with Miss Dawson and Mr. Jaxon. Can you arrange an escort for us?"

Greer looked troubled. "I'm afraid it can't be done, sir. We have the strictest orders. No troops are to cross the deadline set by Red Sleeves until Saturday morning, when we get general marching orders."

Dominick looked grave. "I had forgotten. Of course you're right."

"I can escort Miss Dawson and Mr. Jaxon to our headquarters where they'll be quite safe," Greer said.

"It's important they should be in New York," said Dominick sharply. "I've got to get them there somehow. They've got to be on hand."

Greer looked at Angela and the color flushed up into his cheeks. "I don't like to disagree, sir, but I don't think Miss Dawson should run the risk of trying to get past the Red Sleeve sentries."

"I don't care what you think, Lieutenant," rapped Dominick. "There are issues involved here that would take a month for me to explain. But it's New York for the three of us—and quick!"

Greer looked fussed. He shuffled his boots in the gravel of the roadway. "We've got a car here, sir—armor plated—bulletproof glass—loophole for a machine gun out the back seat. It belonged to some racketeers. The government took it over. I'll take off the army plates, sir. We can put on the ones from this touring car of yours. You might be able to make a run for it."

"Can you supply us with a machine gun—revolvers?"

"It's against regulations, sir, but I'll risk it!"

"Hurry!" was all that Dominick said.

He stood gaunt, grim, staring at the smoldering remains of the building as the plates on the car were changed. Thirty hours! Thirty hours to find Ellison and the others and spoil their game—to founder a revolution!

Greer touched his arm. "Ready, sir."

Dominick turned toward the bulletproof limousine. A rapid-fire gun was set up in the back seat. "Can you use one of those, Philip?" he asked.

"I never have."

"Then drive," said Dominick. "Angela, you ride in front with Philip. If there's any shooting to do I need elbow room!" And then he turned abruptly to Greer. His voice softened a trifle. "Take care of Harbold's body, Lieutenant. If by any wild chance we have luck… Johnny Harbold is the man who did it!" He climbed into the back seat of the limousine. Greer slammed the door.

"Good luck, sir." He saluted.

"Get going," said Dominick to Philip.

BRILLIANT HEADLIGHTS bored into the night, a high-powered motor hummed. They drove in silence, Philip gripping the wheel grimly, his eyes straight to the front. They were driving at a terrific speed. No need to worry about speed cops or traffic. After they swung into the Bronx River Parkway they didn't meet a car. People were not motoring for pleasure these dangerous nights. Once as they passed a police booth Dominick caught a glimpse of Red Sleeve soldiers—a man at the telephone. They would be phoning ahead to the bridge on upper Broadway. That's where the blockade would be.

Now, they were off the Parkway, winding sharply down through Van Cortlandt. Soon they were on upper Broadway. A scant few blocks and they would come face to face with the enemy.

Dominick took a heavy motor robe from a rack in the rear. "Take this," he told Angela. "Wrap it around your head and get down on the floor of the car. If we have a smash-up it may save you a bad injury. Philip, don't stop for anything—men or barriers! Smash through! We've got to get past for me to be able to use this gun."

"Right!" agreed Philip, between his teeth.

The big car was careening in and out of elevated posts. Ahead of them the bridge loomed. Perhaps fifty Red Sleeve soldiers were on either side of the entry. Machine guns were set up. Dominick crouched tensely by his gun.

"Give her everything she's got, Philip!" he said.

Tires screamed as they swung around a post; the car lurched and then drove straight ahead at the armed men. Dominick's nerves were steady as stone as he waited for them to open fire.

And nothing happened!

The gray-uniformed men moved back to make way. An officer in charge saluted! They raced across the bridge without a single shot being sent after them.

"Holy Saints!" Dominick was laughing. "The plates! The number plates off that touring car of Ellison's! They cleared the way for us. Those men up the line phoned ahead and had them clear the way!"

CHAPTER XX

IN TWENTY-FOUR HOURS....

IN THE HOUSE on Fifth Avenue the Red Sleeve High Command was gathered. There were grave faces among those present. Corbett and Frampton, the two millionaires, were showing signs of wear and tear. The big rangy oilman paced the floor of Ellison's office, his hands locked behind his back, knuckles white. Corbett was huddled in a chair, biting restlessly at his fingernails. The pressure was on.

Half an hour before they had arrived from the house they had abandoned in Westchester. Now Ellison, Dawson and Brace were in a huddle. Corbett and Frampton were in this deal—yet strangely out of it. The three leaders were going over reports from various parts of the country. Dawson, still suave, still utterly calm, was reading them aloud:

"*Cincinnati, Ohio—At six P.M. tonight a large force of loyal citizens, armed from sources we have not been able to ascertain, made a fierce attack on the broadcasting buildings of the national radio plant. So savage was the attack it was necessary for commander in charge to order gas attack. Special tanks of X2 were turned on attackers. Almost one hundred percent casualties resulted. Regrettably, citizens living within radius of half mile were killed in large numbers by fumes. Considerable indignation all over city as news spreads. Commander felt justified in taking extreme measures knowing importance of radio plant to our transcontinental radio set-up.*"

Ellison brought his fist down sharply on the desk. "The fools!"

he snarled. "Better to blow the plant to hell than to turn that gas loose on innocent citizens."

Dawson tugged at his gray mustache and read on, in that calm, even voice:

"San Francisco—Mass meeting of loyal citizens successfully broken up by our men. Ringleaders beaten or killed. Casualties on both sides negligible. Radio and newspaper outlets for propaganda well under control.

"St. Louis—Troops and police withdrawn as result of Red Sleeve ultimatum. However, huge forces of mechanized cavalry connected to Third Army Unit laying wide net around the city. Reported that artillery bases are being set up within range of city. Can you inform us if government is bluffing or if they intend to fight?

"Chicago—Huge anti-Red Sleeve gathering made up almost entirely of women belonging to patriotic and peace organizations. Officers deemed it inadvisable to use force in breaking up meetings. Used portable loudspeakers to drown out speeches. Two of these wrecked as women made hysterical attack. Men were weeded out of crowd and beaten.

"And so it goes," continued H.R. Dawson quietly. "There seem to be demonstrations in a great many places. Ah, here's something a little better:

"Pittsburgh—Four men identified as belonging to government intelligence service shot today. Feeling in coal-mining districts and factories strongly in favor of Red Sleeves. Homes of wealthy owners have been sacked. No report as to casualties."

PAUL FRAMPTON could contain himself no longer. "Look here, Dawson, what are you going to do about all these demonstrations against us? What difference does it make if the coal miners and factory workers are for us? They've always been on the left, haven't they? We've been stalling for two days. Why hasn't Ellison moved on Washington? What are we waiting for?"

Ellison cut him short: "Just a minute, Frampton. The government troops can't take New York or any other city we control!

They may do a lot of damage but we can hold *anything* once we turn loose this gas of ours!"

"And commit suicide ourselves!" Frampton cried, shaken.

"Don't be a fool," the general snapped. "We've been soft-pedaling as much as we can because we don't want any more bloodshed than is necessary. We want the people with us. And when they are we won't have to worry about government troops. What's a little shell fire? What are a few airplane raids? We control the main bases of supplies, don't we? They can't feed armies off the countryside forever! We've got railroads in our control. Wait till their army and navy have done a little starving and then we'll see how tough they are. We can stand the gaff. But they won't be able to!"

"I saw those battleships in the harbor when we came in," said Frampton, sucking in his breath between his teeth. "When they open fire...."

"They'll blow down a lot of tall buildings on their own people," said Ellison sharply. "Look, Frampton, if you're going to have a case of nerves, go somewhere else to have it."

Lefty Brace cleared his throat. A cigarette dangled between his lips and his shrewd eyes were fixed thoughtfully on the big glass chandelier overhead.

"It seems to me," he said, "that this would be a swell spot for a smart move." Nobody spoke. Apparently they all had a good deal of respect for this little redheaded man who had done so much of their planning for them. Brace flicked the ash from his cigarette and went on. "Everything the general says is true. We don't have to worry much about force. But we do have to worry about public feeling. The President has issued his Proclamation. It's a pretty fine, high-sounding piece of business. '... sworn to uphold the constitution and will do so with men and guns....' And all that hooey. Well, maybe he'll take a shot at it. And if he does—win, lose or draw—people are going to have a feeling of admiration for him." Brace looked around at them and grinned.

"Now here's my idea and it's a honey. Let's assume, for the

moment, that Saturday morning the government forces will attack. Now suppose, tomorrow, before that attack the General here addresses a huge mass meeting in New York with a nation wide radio hook-up. Let him talk to 'em like a father. We've got our high-sounding phrases too. '*America for Americans.*' We are for the people. We want to lift the yoke of capitalistic oppression and political skullduggery from their necks. We don't want bloodshed unless it is forced on us. But if it is forced on us—if the government attacks—the awful loss of life resulting will not be our fault. Now—let Ellison make an appeal to the people for peace! Let him point out that, for all his oratory, the President is really just trying to keep himself in office!" Brace paused and glanced at the general.

"We're selling you to the people, General. And what could be better than for you to make this appeal to them on the eve of a great catastrophe which your enemies are about to bring on the people!" He looked around him. "Well, how do you like it?"

"I think it's a splendid idea, Brace," said Ellison. "It will swing many people our way; and if the attack comes we will have planted the notion in their minds that it is the government that is at fault. I believe we'll get millions of additional supporters."

Brace checked a smile. "I thought you'd see it that way, General." He looked at Dawson. These two knew the general's weakness for the limelight, but they also knew the power of his impassioned and very sincere oratory.

Dawson nodded slowly. "It has my okay, Brace."

"We'll draw it as fine as we can," said Brace. "Hold it late tomorrow night, just a few hours before the threatened attack. It'll leave no time for any kind of counter-propaganda. I suggest Central Park for the mass meeting. We'll have a platform, huge amplifiers, and our engineers can arrange to bring the speech into every home in the country. All the people are listening to their radios these days."

Dawson chuckled. "It's really a stroke of genius," he said.

JUST ABOUT the time when Lefty Brace was proposing his

great propaganda scheme, a bullet-proof limousine drew up opposite the side-street rectory of one of Fifth Avenues most famous churches. It must have been a strange sight, if there was anyone to see it, when the three occupants of the car got out and headed for the door to the rectory, one of them bringing up the rear with a rapid fire gun held firmly in his hands. Dominick was on the lookout for anything, but the way was clear. It was he who rang the bell that a frightened-looking maid answered.

"Tell Doctor Pancote that I must see him at once," said Dominick.

The maid stood rooted to the floor, staring horrorstruck at the machine gun.

"Hurry!" Dominick said harshly. He herded Angela and Philip into the vestibule and closed the door behind them. The maid turned on her heel and literally ran.

A moment later a kindly old man of about seventy, dressed in the black garb and white collar of his profession came out to them. He had a deeply-lined face, a very firm mouth, and gentle, tragic eyes, but eyes that could, upon occasion, flash fire. He looked puzzled for an instant and then his face brightened.

"Dominick Vane!"

"Doctor Pancote, I've come here because I'm in trouble."

"You're always welcome for any reason, my son," said the minister gently.

"Miss Dawson, Mr. Jaxon—this is Doctor Pancote. He was my chaplain overseas. A grander guy never lived."

"Come in, all of you. I'll call Mrs. Pancote. She hasn't been well. The dreadful state of things, Dominick! Several of the young men in my parish have been murdered."

"Doctor, there isn't time for talk," said Dominick. "It's been so long since I've seen you. I've got to cover a lot of ground. I'm a government agent these days. Right now I have a fighting chance to crack this revolution wide open!"

"Praise God!" said the old man reverently.

"These two young people are terribly important to the government cause, Doctor. So important that if they were to fall into the hands of the revolutionists they would probably be killed on the spot. For reasons which they will explain to you after I'm gone, I must keep them in New York! I've been wracking my brain to think of a safe place. I thought of you. As far as I know there has been no attack on men of your cloth. Will you keep them hidden here, Doctor, until I need them?"

"They can stay here and welcome."

"I must warn you, Doctor, it may be dangerous. If it is found out that they are here…."

The old man held up his hand. "I have hoped a way would show itself for me to serve. I am very proud to have this trust placed in me, my son."

"You must warn every member of your household not to mention their presence. In these days, Doctor, you cannot trust *anyone*. And you two," he said, turning to Philip and Angela, "— if the Doctor has callers, stay out of sight. And be ready when I need you. Get as much rest as you possibly can, you two. And now I'm off."

He turned, stopped abruptly, and turned back. "Angela," he said. For a moment she was in his arms. For a moment her lips were against his.

"God keep you, my darling," she whispered.

"And you," said Dominick—and was gone.

A LITTLE later the incriminating limousine had been deserted blocks from the rectory, and Dominick was hurrying across town toward the public library. In fifteen minutes its doors would be closed and he would have to wait till morning if he were to collect any messages that might have been left by Dugan or Ives.

He just made it and he was still panting for breath when he took down Volume II of the *Decline and Fall of the Roman Empire* and began to ruffle through its pages. Presently his pulse quickened. He had come upon a rather lengthy annotation in one of the margins. Dugan! A message written that day—only ten minutes before!

As he read his eyes picked out key words here and there:— *mass meeting—Ellison—hope to swing millions to cause before attack—last minute—no chance for government propaganda to follow—don't dare try getting information through myself—being followed—*

THE WATCH on the deck of a destroyer off Forty-second Street leaned over the rail, listening. Presently he stood erect and loosened the revolver in the holster at his side. He called softly to the officer of the watch who stood a little farther down the deck.

"Someone swimming toward us, sir."

The strokes of a swimmer were clearly audible now drawing closer in the darkness. The officer and the sailor stood with weapons ready as the swimmer came alongside, gripped the edge of the lowered gangway, and pulled himself out of the water.

"Stay where you are," said the officer, "if you don't want a bullet in your head."

The swimmer raised his hands, but came up the ladder. "Put away those guns and take me to your commanding officer," he said in a voice of authority.

"What's your business?"

"I haven't time to answer questions," said the swimmer. "Put me in irons, do anything you please, but take me to your commanding officer!"

A few minutes later the dripping wet man was ushered into the commandant's cabin.

"My name is Dominick Vane," he said. "Possibly you know who I am. I need your help—and at once."

Three-quarters of an hour later Dominick, in dry clothes, with a heavy navy overcoat covering him, stood on the deck of an airplane-carrier down the harbor. The motor of a plane on the deck roared lustily. Presently the pilot signaled Dominick and he pulled himself up into the observer's cockpit. A moment later they were in the sky, headed through the starless night toward Washington.

Twenty-six hours left!

THE WHITE HOUSE,

Washington, D. C.

A very imperfect method of communication had been established between the nation's capitol and the threatened metropolis on Manhattan Island. The battleships, waiting in New York harbor for the President's order to commence firing, were broadcasting messages by wireless in secret code to the Navy Department in Washington. There was little enough for them to report. Strict orders from the President made it impossible for any men to go ashore, although agents from the Department of Naval Intelligence were at work. However, there was little news coming out of the city—except the bad news that it was sewed-up tight by the Red Sleeves.

But this night a message came which sent the powers that be scurrying to the President's study in the White House. Dominick Vane was on his way from New York with vital information. Corcoran, General Barrett, Admiral Hewitt, the members of the President's cabinet—all waited for the man on whom their waning hope rested.

It was after midnight when Vane arrived in Washington to find himself met by an enormous escort of motorcycle police, state troopers, and an army car with guards on the running boards. The administration was taking no chances of his running into danger between the landing field and the conference room.

Corcoran had managed it so that he was standing near the door when Vane came into the study.

"You're okay, Nick?"

"Okay, Corky." And these two men who had fought shoulder to shoulder for so long looked deep into each other's eyes for an instant.

"I knew you would be," he said.

Then Dominick crossed to where the President waited. He was shocked to see the change in the Chief Executive. The man seemed twenty years older. He leaned with one hand on his desk, as if his legs were too weak to support him. And in his hollow eyes there was a light of such pathetic eagerness that Dominick felt the muscles of his throat contract painfully. But the President's voice was quite steady as he said, "Well, Vane…?"

Dominick swallowed hard. "Mr. President, I wish I could report complete success to you, but I can't. The thing that has brought me here is not news that will help you. Ellison and his smart friends have thought of a really brilliant coup. Tomorrow night, only an hour or two before you must give the signal to attack, they plan a mammoth mass meeting in Central Park with a nation-wide radio hook-up. Ellison is going to speak to America! And when he gets through, Mr. President, he will have thrown the blame for anything that may happen on you. He will have done it convincingly, and will probably add millions of supporters to his cause. Unless we can do something to counteract this before it happens I feel it will be far more serious than the most brilliant Red Sleeve military victory could be."

Slowly the President went around and sat down behind his desk. For a moment his face was buried in his hands.

VANE LEANED forward, his hands on the desk. "Don't give up, sir. I've found out some extraordinary things. There are actually contracts between Ellison and his financial backers. Or rather there were. They may be destroyed now, because Ellison knows that I know about them. But I have two witnesses, safely hidden away, who saw them with their own eyes. If we can find the right moment and the right method we may yet be able to convince the people of what lies behind all this." Quickly, Dominick told them of his adventures as a prisoner of the Red Sleeve High Command. The President listened dully.

"Twenty-four hours! It can't be done, Vane."

"That's my job, sir, and I'm not giving up on it. But I can't impress too seriously the necessity for counteracting this mighty propaganda stunt of Ellison's."

The President looked at him wearily. "How, Vane—how? The Red Sleeves control all the great radio chains—all the newspapers of important. There isn't time to print paper again and fly it over cities. And it wouldn't be effective again. We can't do anything without radio. It is the one direct way to the people."

"Then why not use it?" said a sharp voice. Everyone turned to look at Corcoran who still stood by the door. The color had faded out of his face but his eyes were bright as burning torches. He took three stiff strides toward the President.

"Mr. President, no man has the right to ask another man to risk his life for any cause whatsoever. But I believe, in your heart, you would gladly risk yours if it would save the country."

The President nodded.

Corcoran's voice shook with excitement as he went on. "They're pulling a grandstand play on us, Mr. President. But we, too, could make a play—one that would make theirs insignificant."

"Well, Corcoran?"

"Tomorrow night, Mr. President, tens of thousands of people will assemble in the Park to hear Ellison speak. Millions of people all over the country will be listening at their radios. What would happen, Mr. President, if, instead of Ellison, *you* addressed that throng—spoke over the air to those millions?"

"Corcoran! *How?*"

"It could be done," said the grim-faced Irishman. "They'll be welcoming people into that park to hear Ellison speak. We could crowd a thousand—five thousand—armed men into that mob. At the crucial moment you go up on the platform. *You* speak to those waiting people. Let Dominick produce his witnesses in *that* setting!"

"They'd mob the President before he could open his mouth!" Barrett said.

"Not with our five thousand armed men in that crowd," said

Corcoran. "There'd be danger of a stray assassin's bullet, but you'd have to risk that, sir."

"Ellison will have a huge armed force there to protect him," Barrett said.

"I doubt it," said Corcoran. "It will be only a few hours before they expect our attack. Ellison won't dare take many men away from their critical posts. They'll figure that five hundred or a thousand armed troops will be enough to guard him against any demonstration from a civilian mob."

The President was staring at Corcoran. "And even if I were to die there, making an honest effort to get the truth before the people," he said, "it might turn the tide of battle."

"It would!" said Corcoran.

The Secretary of State laughed harshly. "It's a wild Irishman's pipe dream, Mr. President. We can't let you risk your life."

The President looked at him with a faint smile. "It's my life, Mr. Secretary," he said very softly. "Who has a better right to risk it, or a better cause to risk it for?"

CHAPTER XXI

REUNION ON FORTY-EIGHTH

CORCORAN WENT BACK to the flying field with Dominick. Both men were trembling with excitement.

"It's a tremendous idea, Corky! Magnificent! But I'm afraid he's almost certain to be killed!" Dominick said.

"There's a chance he won't," said Corcoran grimly. "We've got to see to that. You still might get your hands on those contracts if they exist now. But if you can't, it's vital you have Jaxon and Miss Dawson there to speak their piece. Those contracts—or witnesses to the fact that they once existed—are vital."

"I know," said Dominick.

"Guard those kids with your life, Nick," said Corcoran. "The chances are a thousand to one the contracts were destroyed after you escaped from that place in Westchester."

Dominick's hand went out and gripped Corcoran's arm tightly. "Can you picture it, Corky! Can you picture that grand guy back there, willing to step up there in the face of almost certain death! Can you picture what will happen when the people hear him and realize what he's risked for them?"

Corcoran laughed shortly. "Hell, I *did* picture it, didn't I?"

Pilot and plane were waiting for Dominick at the field. Corcoran shook his hand warmly just before he climbed into his seat.

"Barrett and Hewitt and I will arrange getting the President there; and for our bunch in the crowd. All you have to do, Nick,

is produce either the contracts or the kids or both! That ought to be easy after what you've been through."

"Count on it!" Dominick shouted over the roar of the motor.

"Utmost secrecy," Corcoran was yelling as Dominick climbed into the plane. "If a word of it leaks out our goose is cooked."

Dominick's spirits were high on the trip back to New York. He was proud of his friend Corcoran; proud of that great man in the White House who had quickly seized the chance offered him, despite its danger. And he had hope—great hope—for the success of the scheme. American people are easily moved, and tremendously stirred by courage. Well, tomorrow night they'd be stirred to their boot tops. And they'd learn the real truth, they'd hear of the type of men behind the revolution.

It was nearly five in the morning when the plane dropped lightly on the deck of the airplane carrier. The commander of the ship was there to greet him.

"Successful trip?"

"Very," said Dominick.

The commander looked over toward the city. For the first time Dominick noticed that there were strange red flares dotting the sky line all over the town… fires!

"Some sort of terrorist business going on there," said the commander grimly. "We've only got vague reports."

Dominick scowled. "Terrorist?"

"I don't know what's up," said the commander, "but it seems the Red Sleeves have squads out putting the bee on all public men who are known to be against them. Politicians, lawyers, doctors, even priests, our men hear. Anyone who has any influence with crowds of people. I gather they have some big propaganda stunt in mind and are silencing the boys who might do 'em harm before they spring it."

Dominick felt a premonition of danger.

Even priests! "Can you get me a boat to take me ashore quickly?"

ALMOST THE first thing Dominick saw when he got ashore turned his stomach and left him weak and dizzy. A corner saloon, lights blazing, was full of men, loud, drunken, crazy. They were singing and waving their glasses at a grisly object that hung from the chandelier in the center of the place.

It was the body of a man, a rope tight around his neck, dead.

Dominick plunged on across town. In the space of ten blocks he saw three more victims of cold-blooded murder. A doctor, a lawyer, a politician whom Dominick had once known—shot to death on their doorsteps. They had been shot because Ellison was going to speak! And men who were loyalists, who had influence with the people would do everything they could to discredit him before his speech came off! The Red Sleeves were taking no chances.

As he got nearer to Doctor Pancote's house Dominick found himself almost running. Doctor Pancote was a rabid loyalist. If they knew that—a man with two or three thousand people in his church!

Dominick was running now—down the last block toward the rectory. And then, as he swung around toward the front door he stopped dead in his tracks. His fingers reached up to loosen his collar which was suddenly choking him. He tried to move, but for a moment his muscles were dough that he could not control.

The door to the rectory was open. Lying across the doorsill was Doctor Pancote. The silvery white hair had an ugly crimson stain at the base of the skull. Dominick knew, by the grotesque way one arm was twisted under the body, that the old rector was dead.

Then energy came pounding back into Dominick's body. He leaped over the doctor's body, through the door, into the house.

"Angela! Philip! *Angela!*"

Dead silence—and then a groan. Dominick spun around. That sound had come from the next room. He wrenched open the door, stepped across the threshold.

"Philip!"

Philip Jaxon lay face down on the floor. His fingers were clutching at the carpet as if he had been trying to pull himself forward. Quickly Dominick lifted him to a couch in the corner. There was a bullet wound in his shoulder. Another grazing wound on the side of his head. Neither was particularly serious but the boy had lost much blood.

"Philip!! Where's Angela?"

Philip's eyelids fluttered open and he looked up into Dominick's face. "Dominick," he muttered.

"Where's Angela?" Dominick demanded harshly.

Philip's lips trembled and there was a look of terror in his heavy-lidded eyes.

"Moxelli!" he whispered.

SOMETHING SNAPPED in Dominick's head as Philip whispered the name of the Red Sleeve terrorist. He sprang up from beside the couch and started for the door. He could hear the sound of his own voice in a sort of frenzied cry—meaningless—full of anguish and hate and insane murderous fury. At the door some last vestige of sanity checked him, like a tiny steel wire holding tack a load ten times too big. He couldn't leave Philip here to bleed to death! He must take care of him first.

For a minute he stood, looking about him helplessly, as if he expected the room to offer up the solution to his problem. Then he was running again, upstairs, along a corridor, opening doors.

At last! He wrenched open the door of the medicine cabinet in the bathroom. His fingers were stiff, they refused to function for him. Bottles toppled off the shelf to smash in the porcelain basin in front of him. Was there nothing here? No bandages? No disinfectant?

At last he found something—cotton, towels, mercurochrome. Then he leaped down the stairs to the room where Philip lay.

"Easy… easy," he heard himself saying to Philip as he poured the red liquid into the shoulder wound. He knew his hands were rough as he staunched the flow of blood with cotton and wrapped towels around it. But he had to be rough. His muscles were like bats of iron, unpliable.

"Philip! Philip—do you hear me?" he was shouting. "I've got to leave you here. Do you understand? They won't come back! They think they've finished here. *Philip!*" His fingers bit savagely into the unwounded shoulder. "Open your eyes and listen to me!"

Philip had fainted.

Once more Dominick ran. He couldn't seem to avoid furniture. He smashed into chairs, kicked them aside. Like a horrible caricature the vision of Moxelli's thick-lipped, sensuous, leering face was before him. He was in the kitchen of the rectory now, pulling open the doors in front of shelves. At last he found what he had been looking for. A bottle of brandy, almost empty, but enough. In the icebox was food—a cold roast of lamb, milk. He snatched them out. He stumbled back to Philip. The food he put on a little table beside the couch. The brandy he forced between his lips.

And then he was out on the street—running.

"Stop, you damn fool, and think!" he shouted at himself. Where was he going? For a moment he stood in the middle of the sidewalk, his hands pressed to throbbing temples. "Get hold, Vane! You're acting like a madman! Where would he take her? *Where would he take her?*" Not back to West End Avenue. That address was known and Moxelli would have abandoned it! So where? Where, in the midst of ten millions of people, was he to start looking? It was six o'clock—daylight. He couldn't run around the streets yelling like a maniac. "*Think!* There has to be some logical course of action. Use your head!"

And then it came to him. Not two blocks away was the Mordaunt Hotel. Lefty Brace's hangout. He might be there now, in his room. If he was, Dominick knew he had a chance. And once more he was off. Part of his cunning had returned as the outline of a plan suggested itself. He walked now, calmly, leisurely; he mustn't attract attention. The Mordaunt was a Red Sleeve establishment. He couldn't walk into the lobby and hope to get to Brace without the Red Sleeves being warned. At least one of the clerks there knew Dominick from a previous call. But he remembered the number of Brace's room—1511. He remembered that it was a corner room at the back of the building. There was a chance, a good chance, he told himself.

A FEW minutes later he was climbing up the fire escape through the gray morning light. He counted the floors as he climbed. He couldn't remember whether the Mordaunt had a thirteenth floor. Many hotels skipped that number. Was fifteen eleven really the fifteenth floor or actually only the fourteenth?

Once he looked down and felt a faint sense of nauseating dizziness sweep over him. Well, he was taking a chance that there was no thirteenth! He was crouching on the little platform outside the window that must be Brace's. The window was closed and locked. He edged a little closer and peered in. The window across the way was open—there was an indistinguishable figure asleep on the bed.

Dominick's teeth were clamped tight together. If this wasn't the room he was done for. He looked once more, and this time his heart beat a little faster. Hanging from the bedpost near the sleeper's pillow was a leather holster containing a gun. This was it!

For a single moment Dominick crouched where he was. Then he covered his face with the crook of his left arm, lowered his shoulders, braced himself, and dove like a plunging fullback through the window. Dominick stumbled blindly toward the bed. He had fixed his course and even the momentum of that drive through the window did not alter it. There was a cry from the bed and Brace sat up. But already Dominick had his gun, and with his own gun in one hand and Brace's in the other he covered the startled Red Sleeve leader.

"And now, Mr. Brace, it's my turn," said Dominick, in a voice that had a note of doom in it.

For a moment Brace stared at him, resting rigidly on his elbows, and then very slowly lowered himself back against the pillow. A very faint smile flickered on his lips.

"Damned if I don't think it is," he said softly.

"Where is Moxelli?" Dominick demanded.

Brace's smile broadened. "Ah, so you *want* something, Mr. Vane. That makes this all terribly interesting. I was afraid you might just shoot me and be on your way."

"I haven't any time for chatter, Brace," Dominick said, his voice shaking. "I'm giving you just about thirty seconds to make up your mind to tell me where I can find Moxelli."

Brace laughed, and Dominick's nerves tore at him. But he

stood, steady as a rock. "You couldn't kill me if you wanted to, Vane," said Brace. "It wouldn't be cricket! And I'm sure you're a sportsman. I remember being very touched by your remark that I'd only take a poke at you if your hands were tied. Why don't you drop those guns and see what happens?"

"BRACE," SAID Dominick, and his voice was chilling as cold steel in flesh, "I'm not kidding. I've seen my friends shot down by your men; I've seen an innocent minister of the gospel lying dead on his doorstep; I've seen enough brutality in the last few days to knock any notions of sportsmanship or chivalry I may ever have had out of my head. You've got ten seconds left to tell me where Moxelli is!"

Brace moistened his lips. "You wouldn't dare shoot. You'd have the whole hotel down on your neck."

"No one's paying any attention to gunshots this morning, Brace. They've heard too many of 'em in the last few hours! I'm giving you a chance, Brace. Tell me where Moxelli is and I'll see to it that you live to stand a fair trial. That's all I'm promising."

"Nuts!" said Lefty Brace, grinning.

The gun in Dominick's right hand flashed. Brace screamed and sat bolt upright in bed, clutching a shattered knee.

"Talk!" rapped Dominick. "Where's Moxelli!"

Brace clutched his leg, sweat running off his face, calling Dominick every foul name in the vocabulary of a gutter rat. Grim as an avenging angel Dominick's gun spat flame again. Brace fell back on the pillow, his left arm hanging useless at his side.

"Will you talk?" Dominick asked sharply.

"You've gone mad!" Brace cried. "You can't get away with this!"

"Why not?" Dominick snarled. "You and Moxelli and your lads have. You've no mercy on anyone. An hour ago Moxelli killed one friend of mine, gravely wounded another, and kidnapped Miss Dawson. What makes you think I can't pay my debts in kind, Brace... or that I won't. It's your other leg next—then your other arm. And then if you haven't talked I'm going to drill you straight between the eyes. Look at me Brace! Look into *my* eyes and you'll see that I am not bluffing."

Brace's breath was whistling between his teeth and his face was twisted in an agony of pain.

"There's not a shadow of doubt about it," Dominick went on. "And in about fifteen seconds I'll prove it. You've got just one chance to live, Brace. It may go easy with you if I find Miss Dawson unharmed. But your game is up! In twenty-four hours the whole Red Sleeve cause is going to be smashed to hell!"

But Brace wasn't thinking of causes. He was looking at the unwavering muzzles of Dominick's two guns. In a second one of them would stab at him with flame and agony. His teeth were gritted hard together.

"I don't know where Moxelli is," he said slowly. "But I do know where you'll find him if he's with a woman."

"Hurry!" said Dominick grimly.

"Studio apartment—top floor—nine-ninety-one East Forty-eighth Street."

For a second Dominick stared into Brace's sweating face. He was satisfied. The Red Sleeve's nerve was broken. He was telling the truth. Dominick stepped over to the telephone on the bedside table and ripped out the cord. He stepped into the bathroom and came back with two towels. One of them he tore into strips and with it he lashed Brace's good hand to the head of the bed. The other he tied tightly across the gangster's mouth.

"I want you to be here if I come back," said Dominick. "And I'll be back, Brace, if you haven't told me the truth!"

MOXELLI LAY half sprawling on a couch, his fat stomach jiggling as he laughed. His small pig eyes were looking at the girl who stood with her back to the door of the apartment, panic in her eyes.

"And you can yell your pretty head off, my sweet," Moxelli drawled. "No one is going to pay any attention to you—because there isn't anyone else in the building. And there aren't any windows you can throw yourself out of. Only that skylight, which you can't reach."

Angela stood where she was, motionless. "Why have you brought me here?" she asked.

"Now that's a silly question," Moxelli drawled. "But I'll tell you some of the reasons. One of then is that we are mighty anxious to lay our hands on Mr. Dominick Vane. When he finds you're gone I've got a hunch he might give himself up if—it meant your safety. Another is that Vane got my girl killed. I don't know why I shouldn't get even by taking you for myself. Another is that I like you. And another—but what the hell! It all seems quite simple."

"And you're going to hold me here?"

"And how," said Moxelli, with a broad grin.

"My uncle—" Angela began. "Mr. Dawson—"

"Mr. Dawson is in a funny spot," Moxelli chuckled. "Right now he's in the Union Club pretending with all his might that he's a loyalist. That's just in case there are any rumors floating around. After tonight—well—after tonight he'll be out on the limb with us. He won't dare lift a finger to do anything about you, my sweet. So why don't you settle down and take it easy. You're going to be here for a long time."

Those were the last words that Moxelli, the Red Sleeve terrorist, ever spoke. There was a crash of breaking glass and a great section of the skylight came smashing down into the room. At the same moment there were stabbing flashes of flame. Moxelli never drew his own gun. He may never have known that it was Dominick Vane who poured three bullets into his heart.

Dominick dropped down through the hole he had kicked in the skylight. Angela still stood at the door, the back of her hand pressed against her mouth. When she recognized Dominick she began to slide very slowly down toward the floor. He caught her before she fell.

Dominick held her very close in his arms. For the first time he could remember since he had been a small child he was crying. Angela opened her eyes and looked up into his face.

"Dominick!" she whispered.

"It's all right, darling. Everything is going to be all right," he said. "I'm not going to let you out of my sight again—ever."

"Philip?" she asked.

"I think he'll be all right," said Dominick. "You and I are going to him now. And darling—in a few hours I think, I *believe*, these terrible days are coming to an end."

And Dominick felt that he himself was weak and trembling. The mad fury that had lashed him to the frenzied action of the last hour had sapped his strength to the limit.

CHAPTER XXII

"PEOPLE OF AMERICA!"

THE PRESSURE WAS on the Red Sleeve High Command. Dominick would not have found Lefty Brace had he gone back to the Mordaunt after him. General Ellison, unable to reach his chief of intelligence at this critical time, had sent men to the hotel and found him wounded, bound, gagged. They had gotten a doctor for him, and though he was in terrible pain he refused any kind of drug.

"I've got to have the old bean working in the next few hours, doc," he said, between his teeth, as the doctor dressed his wounds. About an hour later he was brought to the Red Sleeve headquarters on Fifth Avenue on a stretcher.

The business of paving the way for the Red Sleeve Broadcast that night was already under way. It was being announced over radio all over the country that General Ellison would speak at exactly ten-thirty that night. Newspapers carried streamers about it. Radio engineers were busy setting up amplifiers on an improvised bandstand in the park and arranging for the radio hookup.

The appearance of Brace, his leg broken, his left arm useless threw the headquarters into a high state of excitement.

"What's happened to you?" Ellison demanded.

"Vane!" said Brace dryly. A cigarette dangled between his lips. He was propped up on pillows.

"How did he find you?"

"Stupidity on my part," said Brace grimly. "Before things

started he knew I lived at the Mordaunt. I figured it was safe enough to stay there in spite of that. Everybody in the hotel is in our pay. He came up the fire escape and—well—you see what happened!"

Ellison glared at him from under his shaggy eyebrows. "But why this crippling? That's not like him. If he'd killed you outright...."

Brace studied the end of his cigarette. "He wanted me to talk."

The general's fist was clenched. "Did you?"

Brace inhaled smoke deep into his lungs. "I have to report, general, that it is extremely doubtful if you will ever see our friend Moxelli alive again."

"You mean...?"

"I mean that I told Vane where he could find Moxelli. Moxelli is—or perhaps I should say 'was'—a fool, general. We sent him out last night to quietly eliminate a few undesirables. He makes a bloody massacre of it. He stumbles across the Dawson girl. Does he bring her here to headquarters? No, he takes her to a hideout of his. Vane wanted to know where that hideout was. In the end I decided I'd better tell him because otherwise he would have killed me. I thought you needed me more than you needed Moxelli."

For a moment Ellison was silent. "You did the right thing," he said finally. "You should have told him sooner. I can't afford to lose you now."

"Don't worry," said Brace. "From now on I stay right here with plenty of guards around me. About tonight—is everything under way?"

"It is." Ellison was scowling darkly. "I've been wondering what move the government will make when they learn what's coming. It's occurred to me the President may give the order to attack *before* our broadcasting time. I have ordered patrols out on the roads to report any sign of troop movements. I have redoubled the number of our chemical stations. If there is the slightest movement against us I've given orders for the men to commence a gas attack at once."

Brace nodded and winced as pain shot along his arm. "About your own personal bodyguard, General. Moxelli's tough guys are good, but they are not impressive. I suggest our best-drilled regiment, done up as smartly as possible. This is a show, General, and don't forget it. We're out to impress."

"You're right, of course," said Ellison.

"I'll have four or five hundred of our best strong-arm boys circulating in the crowd," Brace went on, "but the uniformed men I think, must be our best-drilled unit." He chuckled. "I've got a hunch when you get through playing the great white father tonight, the country is going to fall plop into your lap, General. My only disappointment is that I won't be able to be on hand."

IT WAS a strange, tense day all over America. The news that Ellison was to make a nationwide appeal seemed to have put a stop to all sporadic outbursts of the loyalists. They were waiting to hear what the Red Sleeve leader had to say. And in the background was the menace of a terrible and bloody conflict to come. At any moment after midnight the government forces, waiting ominously quiet outside the limits of many of the big cities, might attack. The greatest panic centers were New York, St. Louis, and Los Angeles. Here the greatest concentration of government forces lay in wait. Citizens found themselves unable to leave because of Red Sleeve blockades. They could do nothing but wait for the explosion. And it seemed that it must come. The Red Sleeves were riding the crest of success. If the government failed to strike now after this three-day wait, they were done for. Everyone knew that. And everyone knew that the man in the White House was not going to give up without a fierce struggle!

Citizens stayed indoors. Mothers hovered over their children. Families clung together as if they realized that this was the last moment of peace before a tornado.

As early as six o'clock that night people began crowding around radios. In rural centers country stores were jammed.

Outside New York men foregathered in bars and restaurants to listen; families waited tensely in their homes. There might be some change in the time schedule. It was rumored that Ellison would offer terms of peace with the Federal Government; it was rumored that he would agree to let people leave the storm centers before the hour of attack; it was rumored that the President was dead—that this broadcast would really be the announcement that Ellison had taken over the reins of control.

There were other places where the tension was even greater. In the battered rectory near Fifth Avenue Dominick and Angela had spent the day tending to Philip. Philip was going to be all right, but Philip was not going to be able to attend that broadcast in the park. If testimony about the contracts was to be given, Angela must give it alone. And she was willing. But cold fear gripped Dominick's heart. If anything happened to her again, if she were shot as she stood up on the platform to speak… He had given up all hope of getting the contracts themselves even if they still existed. He dared not leave Angela. And so they must wait—wait for hours until that moment when she would step forward to tell what she knew.

And there was tension in the mess of one of the battleships in the harbor.

At the head of the table sat the President of the United States. He had been whisked up from Washington in a plane and hidden on this boat. He seemed alone… terribly alone. Corcoran, Barrett and Hewitt, his chief aides had slipped ashore. They were arranging for the evening's events. The officers at the table knew what was to take place. Somehow they could not talk.

Calmly the President ate. From time to time he tried to stir the others into some kind of conversation. Always it died down as it began—with the President himself. In a little more than three hours he would go before the American people—would probably sacrifice his life—in an attempt to reach them with the truth. He was quite calm. There were high spots of color in his cheeks. Somehow, with action at hand, he seemed to have thrown off his weariness and despair.

He took a stroll on deck with the commander after dinner. Their cigars glowed red in the darkness. From time to time the President looked across the black waters at the lights of the Manhattan, where presently he must face his destiny.

Once he spoke. "I have only one hope," he said very gently. "That they will listen to me before they kill me!"

"You mustn't talk that way, sir!"

The President paused, listening. "I think I hear the launch coming, Commander. That means I'll be going ashore presently. I—I should like to have a few minutes alone in my stateroom before we go."

BY SIX o'clock that night people had begun to gather in the Park. There were thousands upon thousands who wanted a glimpse of Ellison in the flesh; the man who seemed destined, by force of arms, to be the next ruler of their country. A barbed-wire pen had been built around the platform on which the General would stand to make his speech, and already, inside this barrier, Red Sleeve soldiers waited, machine guns set up and pointing out toward the crowd.

Men, women, even children were taking up points of vantage near the front of the platform. Great amplifiers towered over the platform; engineers were still working on the radio hookup, testing microphones, making certain that everything would be perfect for the Red Sleeve leader when his moment came.

And as the crowd grew in size, its citizen body was perhaps unaware that hundreds of Red Sleeve shock troops were present, dressed in civilian clothes, adroitly bumping and shoving people around for the purpose of discovering anyone who might be armed. Now and then some man was discovered carrying a revolver. Action was quick. His gun was taken away from him; a fist was jammed in his face, and he was hustled out of the throng to be taken into custody by waiting squads of uniformed men. So smoothly did they work, so quickly and sharply, that there was very little disturbance in the crowd.

And still the thousands kept pouring into the great open grass space. By nine-thirty there were probably a half a million people jammed around that platform… a roaring hum of voices… a high-pitched, hysterical laugh here and there… a cry of pain as one of the Red Sleeve undercover men slugged some poor unfortunate and took away his gun.

And in that crowd, close to the speaker's stand, were Dominick and Angela, clinging tightly to each other, nerves keyed almost to the breaking point. Dominick had been unable to get in touch with Corcoran or any of the government men. He had no idea how their plans were progressing. And as he, with his trained eyes, saw the efficiency with which the Red Sleeve undercover men were working his hope waned. Corcoran was going to get no five thousand men in this crowd without the alarm being spread. But he and Angela were there, waiting to answer the call for their services, when and if it came.

"They'll never manage it, Dominick, never!" Angela whispered tensely.

"Hush, darling!" His hand gripped her arm tightly. "You must not even think about it. Everywhere in this crowd are enemy ears and eyes. We must simply wait—and trust Corcoran!"

And then suddenly his muscles went tense. Not five feet away from him was a man whom he had already spotted as one of the Red Sleeve undercover men. He had jostled into a bulky-looking fellow, wearing an overcoat. He started to draw back his fist to slug the man. Then an extraordinary thing happened. The overcoated man's right hand went up… there was a gun in it… and he brought the butt down in a savage blow on the Red Sleeve's head. Then quite calmly he took the unconscious man by the collar and dragged him out through the crowd!

"Look!" Dominick whispered excitedly. "The G-men are here! They're working on the Red Sleeve spies and nobody knows the difference!"

It was true. All through that crowd the Red Sleeves strong-arm men were suddenly having the tables turned on them; one by one. They were being slugged into insensibility. The crowd had seen this weeding-out process going on for hours and there was no outcry.

TEN MINUTES past ten! From out on Broadway the strains of martial music reached the multitude. Ellison was coming! He sat in the back seat of an open touring car, his chin sunk forward on his chest, his burning eyes looking out at the people who lined the streets, cheering and yelling. It was the triumphal procession of a conqueror.

In front and behind Ellison's car marched the crack regiment of Red Sleeve troops, smart, jaunty, precise, bayonets glistening on the end of rifles. Into the entrance of the park they swept. A great avenue was broken open in the waiting throng and the troops marched proudly through to the platform. Here they deployed around it in a huge circle, ten deep. Ellison stood up in the back of the car, his hand outstretched in a salute to the crowd who greeted him with a wild ovation—an ovation over-toned with hysteria. And then he got down, surrounded by guards, and made his way through a gap in the wire barricade to the platform.

And at that moment Dominick felt a hand on his arm and he looked up into the face of General Barrett, dressed in civilian clothes.

"Get in as close to the platform as you can," said Barrett grimly. "The minute we take over you and Miss Dawson are to make for the platform." And before Dominick could speak, Barrett was gone in the crowd again.

A man was coming across the platform toward the microphones. Dominick recognized him as a former labor agitator. He held his hands high above his head for silence. The result was extraordinary.

A half a million people were suddenly standing dead still—listening. Dominick felt suffocated by that strange quiet. He knew that at that moment millions and millions of people all over the land were sitting tensely at their radios—waiting.

"People of America!" The words boomed out loud and clear

over the vast throng. There was a little murmur of satisfaction as people on the outskirts of the crowd realized that they were going to be able to hear satisfactorily. "In the last week," the speaker said slowly, clearly, "history has been made! A great people have risen up in face of a system that has been crushing out their life blood, and have tossed it aside and trampled it under foot! In these times, my friends, there have been hardships. Many of you have lost friends and relatives! There has been bloodshed! But there can be no great social upheaval without loss of life. The leaders of this great cause have been forced to strike quickly, sharply, and without wavering from their objective. And now, with victory in their grasp, with the tyranny of a corrupt and bureaucratic government at an end, we are faced with a terrible catastrophe brought about by the selfish determination of that government to wreak its vengeance on the people of America.

"Outside this city troops and battleships wait to strike! For what? To keep one man in office—a man who is the representative of capitalism, of corrupt politics, of graft, of oppression. In a vain effort to maintain the old inefficient status-quo, the old rulers are prepared to spill the blood of millions of innocent citizens."

There was a booming roar of anger from the crowd. The speaker held up his hands.

"You have not come here to listen to me! On this platform is a man whose courage, whose ideals, whose great love for his country—these United States which were conceived by our forefathers that their descendants might have a place to live in liberty and freedom—this man, I say, inspired by these ideals, has had the courage to strike a blow for America. It is he who will talk to you now. He will tell you of his dreams and hopes for his country, and of his plans for the future. He will tell you what he intends to do to *protect you* from the murderous plans of the government! People of America, I give you...."

He didn't finish. Ellison had already risen from his chair when the storm broke.

CHAPTER XXIII

ATTEMPT

SUDDENLY THE FRONT of that great crowd that encircled the speakers' stand seemed to sweep forward like a great sighing wave. From under hundreds of overcoats appeared hundreds of rapid-fire guns. A solid phalanx of them were leveled at the troops around the stand. And back to back with these men were an equal number with rapid fire guns leveled at the crowd. It had been done with the speed and precision of a magician's sleight-of-hand trick. Out into the open, between the soldiers and the government men limped Corcoran. A soft-brimmed hat was pulled down over his eyes, and he carried a rapid-fire gun.

"You will drop your rifles in ten seconds or we open fire!" His voice rang clear and steady over the crowd.

Even as he spoke a rapid fire gun belched death from one sector of that grim circle—at Red Sleeve soldiers who had raised rifles to their shoulders. Sudden terror gripped the crowd. People were shouting, screaming, cursing and cheering! On the platform the speaker had reached for a revolver, but there were men swarming up the steps to seize him—to seize Ellison who was tugging at his own gun. Somewhere else from the circle a rapid fire gun raked the ranks of soldiers. A Red Sleeve officer shouted an order to attack and fell as the top of his head was blown off by a government agent. Another rapid-fire gun spoke! It was enough. Rifles clattered to the ground. Red Sleeve soldiers held their hands aloft.

Someone seized Dominick by the arm. It was Barrett again.

He and Angela were whisked through that grim circle to the steps of the platform. Barrett and Admiral Hewitt followed them up. John Dewar, famous liberal senator from the West, was shouting into the microphones for quiet. He was to be the first speaker for the government. Somewhere in the crowd a pistol flashed. Dewar fell, clutching at a wound in his stomach.

Barrett gave Dominick a quick look. "Speak to them, Vane! We're got to hold this crowd until we can get the President up on the platform!"

"But General, I'm not qualified to—"

"*Speak to them!*" Barrett rasped.

And so it was that the first loyalist voice chat went over the microphone to that hysterical crowd and into a million homes was that of Dominick Vane—a man of whom none of them had ever heard—yet a man who had risked his life ten times over for all of them.

Dominick was not an orator. His voice was harsh; yet there was a passionate intensity as he shouted: "*Listen! Listen, all of you!*"

It was a strange picture. That seething crowd, raised to an insane pitch of excitement by the sudden turn of events; the Red Sleeve soldiers with their hands raised; that grim double circle of death covering the platform and the crowd.

"You've been tricked!" Dominick was shouting. "All of you have been tricked. You, who have been followers of General Ellison, have been led to believe that you are fighting for a great cause. That is a lie!"

A thunder of disapproval from the crowd.

"*Listen!* I'm a government agent—I don't deny that! But I'm an American like any of the rest of you. I fought overseas alongside many of you! I'm not holding any brief for our government. I'm here to tell you facts about Ellison and the revolution. They say they are fighting capitalism! Fine! But how have they financed this revolution? I'll tell you how! The men who are paying for this are H.R. Dawson, Paul Frampton, John Corbett and other Wall Street powers!"

There was another roar of derision and disapproval.

"LISTEN!" DOMINICK stormed. "This is not propaganda! For five days I've been fighting to get the proof of this. Would you believe Ellison and the other Red Sleeve leaders were on the level if you knew that they had signed contracts with Dawson and his friends, promising them control of all our natural resources once he is in power? Would you still believe in their high-sounding phrases if I told you that your love for your country is being exploited so that your country can be torn from the hands of those who govern constitutionally and given over to a group of robber barons. I'm going to give you the proof of that. Standing beside me here is a girl—the ward of H.R. Dawson himself. She saw those contracts with her own eyes! You are being sold down the river, People of America! Listen to what this girl has to say!"

Angela was white and trembling. Dominick stood close to her, holding her hand as she spoke. "It is true," she said. "Every word that you have heard is true! Mr. Dawson and his friends have financed this rebellion. They are behind it for their own personal greed. After you have fought and died you will find yourselves the slaves and dupes of these men. There were contracts between Ellison and Mr. Dawson and his friends! I saw them! I read them with my own eyes."

The crowd was muttering. There was a curious low angry buzz. And then Dominick saw a little body of men pushing their way toward the platform. They were permitted to pass through the ranks of the G-men. Dominick seized Angela's hand and pulled her quickly back from the microphone.

"People of America," he shouted, "the first speaker tonight promised to present to you a man who loved his country, a man of high ideals, a man who has the courage to strike a blow, a man with dreams for the future of his country! Well, I am going to present that man to you! He has come here at the risk of his life

to tell you the truth about America! Ladies and gentlemen"—
Dominick's voice shook with emotion—"I give you the President of the United States."

He raised his hand slowly, like a figure in a dream, to brush
sweat from his brow. Until he straightened it by a suddenly
conscious effort, his body slumped with aching fatigue. He
hadn't realized how bone-weary he had become.

Dominick stood back from the microphone and looked out
toward the President. The President wore a heavy overcoat but
he held his hat in his hand and his head was thrown back, the
light from the platform glistening on his gray hair and lighting
his broad calm forehead. There was a dignity about him that did
not arise merely from his erect carriage or the habitual poise of
the man: it came, not from the man, but from those ideals the
man stood for. And the crowd seemed to feel this. For a moment
in the vast quad of the Park none seemed to breathe; there was
no sound but the sound of the President's, and his followers',
footsteps on the trampled grass. And then there was a rustle,
like a wind in a forest, and the crowd stirred and muttered and
some shouted out taunts and some faintly cheered.

The President came slowly forward toward the microphone.
He was pale, but very steady on his feet.

Then bursting out to the front of the crowd came a man. It
was all so quick…. Foul abusive curses came from his twisted,
lips. He fired….

Before he could pull the trigger a second time he was buried
under a stampede of clubbing, frenzied listeners.

On the platform the President staggered. Dominick caught
him before he fell. And for a moment he clung to Dominick,
bent, shaking. Then very slowly he stood erect. Dominick saw
the sweat on his forehead—saw the dark wet stain spreading
on his coat.

Dominick turned quickly to Barrett.

"We've got to get him out of here, General. He's badly hurt."

"No, no!" It was the President speaking. "I came here to speak.
I'm going to speak!"

CHAPTER XXIV

"I AM YOUR SERVANT...."

FURY SWEPT OVER Dominick. He shouted into the loud-speakers: "Listen, all of you! The President is badly hurt! He insists on speaking to you in spite of that. And you're going to listen if we have to turn loose these guns on the whole lot of you."

The President took several unsteady steps toward the microphone and stood there, leaning heavily on Dominick's arm. Even out front it was clear that he was hurt—severely hurt.

And suddenly that great crowd was still again.

"People of the United States of America!" The President's voice was steady, clear as crystal, as it winged its way out over the length and breadth of a nation. "One of the first rights for which our forefathers fought was the right to speak freely. I haven't come here tonight to plead for your support. I have come here because, as your President, I have the *right* to speak to you.

"You have heard a great deal of talk in the last few days. Talk about rights; about causes; about capitalism and oppression. I haven't come here to talk about those things. I have come to talk to you about the one thing that we all have in common—our love for this country in which we live."

Dominick felt the President's fingers biting into his arm. "You can't go on, sir," he whispered. "We've got to get you to a hospital!"

Very gently the President shook his head and continued: "Tonight this great city faces a crisis. It is in the hands of a revo-

lutionary group. Outside the city are government forces ready
to fight if necessary to put down that revolution. But before any
more blood is shed, you must know the truth. What you have
heard here tonight about the leaders of that revolution is true.
I swear that to you. But I do not ask you to take my word, or
the word of Mr. Vane, who has risked his life to get that proof
for you, or the word of this courageous girl who has stood here
before you. I ask you to demand of this revolutionary party to
prove to you that it is *not* so. I know that in your hearts is a dread
of what may happen in the next few hours. I want to relieve
you of that anxiety now. The government forces *will not attack
tonight or tomorrow!*"

A mighty, full-throated murmur went up from the crowd. The
President silenced them with raised hand. Dominick's throat
was choked.

He could feel the strength waning in the frantic clutch the
President had on his arm.

"**WE ARE** going to withhold that attack until you can prove to
your own satisfaction that we are telling you the truth about the
revolutionary leaders. Ask them where the money came from to
arm and equip thousands of troops? Ask them who paid for the
ammunition and poison gas and food and uniforms—millions
and millions of dollars it must have cost. You know and I know it
did not come out of the pockets of workers or any other group of
society. And when you have realized that these men have spilled
the blood of your friends, your families; that they have wrecked
your homes for the sole purpose of getting into power, will you
still shout for their warriors? The troops outside this city are not
your enemies. *They are your troops!* The ships in the harbor are
your ships! They are here to protect *you*. We, who have been put
into power by *you*, believe that the Red Sleeve organization is
a treacherous, an evil, a vicious ring which has led thousands of
citizens astray by false promises, false battle cries. And because
that army and navy is yours, organized for your protection, we
must fight this enemy—the Red Sleeves—who are *your* enemies.

"And what do they bring you—? The meaningless waving of a flag that is defiled by their very touch. The ranting, high-sounding phrases of a patriotism they have dishonored. Vague promises of purely imaginary benefits to all of you which a knowledge of their purpose proves they have no intention of fulfilling."

The President paused. He was weakening rapidly. His face was paper-white; he trembled visibly. But he went on.

"I am not here because I wish power or glory. I am your servant. You elected me to office and I am sworn to serve you. If I could have averted these terrible days by giving my life I would have done so. But that would not serve. And so I have stuck to my guns in the face of your abuse and hatred, because that was the job I promised to do when I took the oath of office to which you elected me." He swayed on his feet and Dominick had to slip an arm around his waist to keep him erect. He knew it was useless to plead with the President to stop until he had finished.

And this was the man his people had so nearly betrayed. This was he who the Red Sleeves said was not fit to govern his country. A tool, they called him… a puppet!

"And I would tell you this—all you Americans!"—Dominick felt the President draw himself up for one last effort—"The men who built the structure of our government were wise men. They made it so that no man can hold office without the complete approval of the people. There is no royal dynasty here. They made it so that revolutions would never be necessary. They gave their lives to set us free from tyranny and they saw a way to avoid the necessity of that sacrifice being made again. You do not have to revolt against the men who rule you with guns and death, my friends. There is no political machine in the world that can exist in the face of defeat at the polls. The reason for political corruption in America today is not because there is a flaw in our scheme of government, but because you do not interest yourselves in government machinery. If there are dishonest and corrupt men in positions of power it is *because you put them there!*

"I pray that these dreadful days will awaken you to your responsibilities as citizens of the greatest of all nations!

"I have promised you that for a time we will stay our hand until you have investigated the truth about the revolutionary leaders. I am sure that thousands of you who have fought for their cause will see that you have been misled and betrayed. I pray that you will then see that what we do to exterminate them we do for you."

"And now"—his whole weight was sagging in Dominick's arms—"I…I leave you. And remember, the soil of your country will never grow rich if it is fertilized by the blood of your brothers. You have been provided with a way of peace to get what you want. I pray that you will choose that way!"

There was a tense silence at the end of that speech. A murmur ran over the crowd as they saw that Dominick and General Barrett had literally to carry the President down from the speakers' stand. And then suddenly, as he was borne out through the crowd, a great cheer went up, to be repeated and repeated, like the roaring of a mighty wave thundering on a rocky shore. The President looked up at Dominick, and there was a smile on his lips.

"Well, Mr. Vane?"

Dominick choked, and his eyes were hot and smarting. "I think you turned the trick, sir."

THROUGHOUT AMERICA, it was a wild night. The President had pleaded for a way of peace, but those early hours were bloody. The chief cause lay in the sudden rebellion of thousands of the revolutionists themselves. General Ellison who had come to Central Park so proudly, did not leave the speakers' stand alive. Dawson, Frampton and Corbett were on the high seas in Dawson's yacht headed for Europe. And while the Red Sleeves snarled at each other's throats the government forces waited calmly outside the city.

But the night, hideous and unbelievable as it was, drew at last to a weary end. Its blackness paled before the light.

At dawn Dominick, Corcoran, Barrett and others waited tensely outside the operating room of a great hospital. Angela sat by a window looking down at the street. Crowds still milled about. Outside the hospital thousands stood waiting for news.

Presently the door of the operating room opened. One of America's greatest surgeons came out, his face gray and tired. He still wore his white operating robe and cap. He looked at the anxious faces and his lips were compressed, tight and thin.

"Gentlemen," he said very quietly, "the President is dead."

There was a tragic silence for a moment, broken by the sound of Angela's sob. A wave of passionate anger swept over Dominick.

"Damn them!" he cried.

Corcoran's hand was on his arm, Corcoran, whose face was rudely lined and set now in a granite-hard mask. He was looking past Dominick... out the window over the rooftops of the city.

"We have fought for a country, not a man," he said. "The President has died for that country, and his death will insure the victory for which he prayed."

The door to the operating room opened and very slowly two internes wheeled out a stretcher. The body of the President rested on it, completely covered by a white sheet.

There was a sharp click as General Barrett's heels snapped together and he raised his hand in stiff salute.

THE ARGOSY LIBRARY ™

SERIES 7 INCLUDES:

* BRAND * TUTTLE * BECHDOLT *

HORN * MCCULLEY * ROSCOE *

* HALL & FLINT *

* BEYER * MCCALL *

* MONTGOMERY *

THE BEST FICTION
FROM THE FRANK
A. MUNSEY LINE

www.ingramcontent.com/pod-product-compliance
Lightning Source LLC
Chambersburg PA
CBHW050528260626
47157CB00004B/1517